I0761754

TRANSPARENT BODY

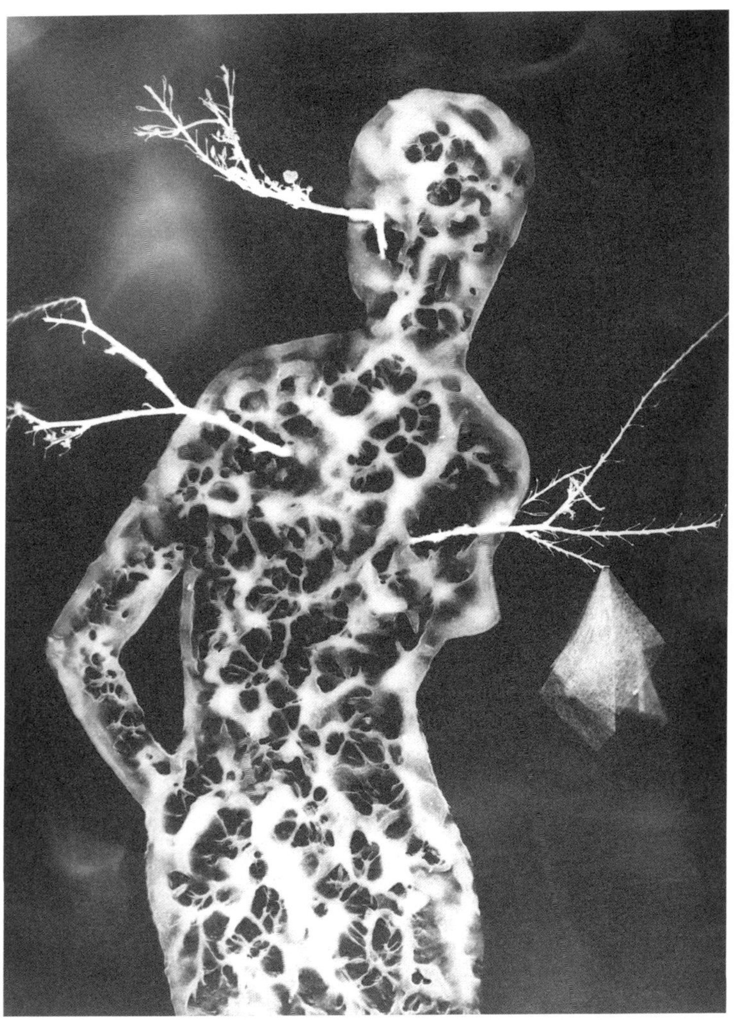

Max Blecher

TRANSPARENT BODY & OTHER TEXTS

Translated from the Romanian by
GABI REIGH

TWISTED SPOON PRESS
PRAGUE
2024

ISBN: 978-80-88628-03-3
ISBN: 978-80-88628-32-3 (e-book)

This publication was made possible by a grant from the Translation and Publication Support Program of the Romanian Cultural Institute, Bucharest.

CONTENTS

SHORT PROSE

TRANSPARENT BODY

to Marie

IN PLACE OF AN INTRODUCTION

Words birds with blood wings
Words manically flapping through the chambers of the heart

Occasional animals with celestial transparence
Bouquets of astral worlds (comets with the heads of dancing girls)

Bizarre flowers perfuming the brain
Signifying a smile or else a joy

Appearing and disappearing into the darkness of days
Or the white flutter of eagles over mountains of sleep

Lunar vitrines filled with angels and swords
With wolves, with cities, with ships, with women's hair

Words, unfathomable pictures of writing
Just like my hands, just like your closed eyes.

ETERNITY

Our footsteps know our abyss
The body hauls our sky
The storm sheds pieces of flesh
Each time less certain, less fierce
A blue beginning
In this terrestrial landscape
And another one, vengeful
Like a severed finger
See the woman who rolls
Like a spindle
Her delta mirroring
The delta of waters.

A POEM

I

The inside of your gaze floats me a skiff
laden with the velvet of black eyes and the tiny diamonds
of so many dreams so many abysses yesterday evening
an angel hanged himself in a moment of happiness
and his fallen wings creak beneath your feet
crushed into snow, flowers, fingers.

II

The dress of the sea inside a sapphire shell you walk or slide
ship or acrobat, you are a vertical stream the diadem
of your blue hair a cascade of ferns or screams
and look, a window tilting, you transform your transparencies
and you're a dead woman a phantom clad in a sea dress
inside a sapphire shell, the palm tree extends its arm and
salutes you, the ships float away with your footsteps and the clouds
glide your beauty towards twilight.

THE HORSE

for Sașa Pană

Stirred by his pride in the hay the horse
On a sunsplashed path of hair
Rises from the earth untethering itself from the earth
Beneath its hooves, snowflakes of dirt drift into the azure
Like a sail on the mast
Of the day
Its mane fans through the sky
The horse is the woman of cameo water
Her breasts are clouds
Her gestures as real as claws
In the brain
A banner of death's faded sleep
An island of the morning cold madness
Like a droplet of mercury on the carpet.
The horse appears the horse disappears
Between the fruit trees
Its ears, zephyr
Its earrings, sparrows
The horse leaps into the world

WALKING

for Pierre Minet

Forever stepping forward the shadows of my footsteps die
Like the tail of a comet in the darkness
And the asphalt I leave behind quells me
With everything that I've once been or thought
Like a conjuror
Intent on making my life disappear.
An orderly string of houses
On this road somehow
Must have some meaning
A colourless scentless meatless sky
Arches above my meaningless footsteps
With closed eyes I walk into a black box
With open eyes I walk into a white box
And no matter how hard I strain to understand
Heavy hammers smash my every thought.

ON THE SHORE

Here is what you will glimpse on the sea
Ships like drowned heads puffing on cigarettes
Dreaming, smoking, steaming towards Istanbul
People on the shore like suicides cheating death
Promenade in the twilight, dreaming and smoking.

MATERIALISATIONS

If only the day were to gift me a stone in a box
And a golden butterfly on the skylight, like stained glass
If only the night were to gift me a handful of crystals
Shattered from an icicle of fever — a toy of dreams
If only I could possess objects forged by the heart
And thoughts weaved in silk and memories etched in glass
From your visits I would glean blood bracelets
The necklace of a smile and the ring of a moment.

A PASTORAL

An expanse of plants with fingers of water
Drink it in and regard
The lacy petticoats of raw milk
The subterranean giants drowned in blue
While the lakes of an open mouth petrify
Four oxes under a tree, defying reality
As they kneel and festoon their horns
With banewort blooms
The perfection of weeping passes through the clouds
And infant lambs suck the teats of the rain
The planet of sleep cloaks the hills
The ripples of streams drain away the last glimmers of light
Like the last lucid words of a dying man
While you brew spells from the ornamental, fatal bones
Of our love.

MOTH LOVE

for Geo Bogza

Moth love of black harbours
Perfumed light of vast tropics
Rumination as long and smooth as a ray, as tormenting as the sea
And the flaming horizon shut tight like a trap

Urban love of shadows rebounding from pavements
And furtive voices buried in death
And hands flicking slowly the pages of useless albums
Afternoon love in blurred shuttered rooms

Love scented with the harshness of clay and seeds
Under the grass, the horse, the heavy-grained summer
Love wept into handkerchiefs or revelled in the sun
With smooth, white skin or ancient hands

Love, web of the world where its captives
Dance like earnest, demented bufoons.

GROTESQUE POEM

for René Wauquier

I

The green soldier who lives on the moon sometimes sends me an orange, sliding on a thread of saliva, sometimes a parsley leaf (a hair plucked from his green beard), and other times his watch with phosphorescent numbers. The watch sinks to the bottom of the sea flapping so wildly that it shatters the waves (boat sails snap like poppers).

Children flying kites in the afternoon tug at a thread of saliva but the soldier sends them nothing at all, no badgers nor dry figs.

II

Musical notes rain on a water gramophone as flour cherubs play on flour trumpets while my elephant's trunk gets tangled in a never-ending spiral without a period or a comma the window has liberated itself from the wall and is making its way through the world, bon voyage because, look, here I'm drawing another window.

MENAGERIE

Here I am, your dog with its fringed coat
And sword teeth to bite you, bark at you
Here I am, your serpent, tempting you
With the sun's apple poisoning you
Here I am, your rhinoceros dressed like a clown
Juggling skittles, making you laugh
Here I am, your giraffe. Uppercase character
In the text of the day, read me as A
Here I am the eagle of sunset
My heart in my beak, lit like a lantern.

YOUR HANDS

Your hands on the piano like two horses
With marble hooves
Your hands on vertebrae like two horses
With rose petal hooves
Your hands in the azure like two birds
With silk wings
Your hands on my head
Like two stones on a single grave.

A POEM

Your shell
Like a bird in the nest of the heart
You bathe in rivers of blood
And fly from the tips of my fingers

When you leave
Your body reclaims its infinite density
And the drunk, open landscape
Signifies your absence

With hands as deep as panniers
You lift me from the ocean of sleep
And my head echoes like a conch shell

You, a stone hurled into a lake
You, ripple of water, abandoning

Waiting for you might resurrect
The corpse of a word
With its blind lantern, guiding me
Through the night

Your hair will be my darkness
And I will lose myself in the shadows.

OLD TIME WALTZ

Old time waltz dead bride veiled in shrouds of dust
Garlands of wan girls in foam dresses
Whirling on the arms of jacks of spades around ashen alleys
Perfuming them with the vague scent of clay

Moon cemetery, acacias lording over shadows
Like distinguished guests attend and secretly whisper
In crypts where forlorn paramours
Confess their love through somnolent gestures.

Old time waltz wax couples rise up in the air
Dancing their dizzying dance in the night's parlour
Everything around me terrifyingly ordinary
The wind idly rustling, the waltz's delirium

It is the wedding day of one who once lived
A wedding when the one who lives dies in flowers of blood
Spectral shudders rippling through her white face
As the slow waltz spins, as the waltz pours into tears.

SEASIDE PROMENADE

for I. Ludo

The sea's blood circulates crimson into coral
The water's sunken heart roars in my ears
I am under the waves' sky
In the cellar of the deep
In the murdered light of funereal glass
Tiny fish, platinum toys,
Comb through the waves of my hair
Giant fish, packs of hounds,
Urgently suck up water. I am alone
I raise my hand and note the liquid heaviness
Recalling a cogwheel, a palm tree
Vainly I try to whistle
As if traversing a melancholy mass
And it is as if everything has always been so
Half beautiful, half sad.

OTHER POEMS

THE INEXTRICABLE POSITION

A deep wound sinks into my chest until it reaches the heart. It is the same ulcer of old, disguised by its new meaning; new aches, new hideousness now bind me to my flesh. A horse echoes my thought or rather a horse's eye, bulging with a minuscule head mirroring the larger one, only more pallid, visibly more tormented (like a fetish doll). As for the rest : I am stripped to the waist, thin cardboard trousers rigidly cover my legs, so that the whole street (irredeemably tied to this moment, just like the horse) will take me for a monk searching for a quiet pocket of air where he can store his rings.

PARIS

You remember when you first arrived, the locomotive rumbling
in your head Paris Paris
It was dark and other darknesses lurked in the streets, in the air,
You pulled tight the collar of your winter coat so that the night
wind could not invade
The gaping hole in your chest, the singular abyss
of your melancholy
The boulevards were as desolate as ancient cemeteries,
Deserted gardens bereft of people invaded only by silences.
You were crying or were on the verge of tears, the sky clouded over,
the same worn sky
The same narrow sky of your provincial sadnesses, the same
worsted cloth sky
You left your suitcase at the hotel, your soul packed away inside
The soul you brought from home, neatly folded between
clothes scented with basil
And wandered out into the streets, soulless, suitcaseless,
fleshless like a phantom
Like a cloud on the asphalt sky, formless and vaporous like a cloud.
Your wildly gesticulating hands knocked against the houses
Hemming the streets where you walked, Paris Paris ringing
in your ears
Until, exhausted, your feet aching your head aching your
shoulders aching
You entered a house lit up like on a feast day; it was a brothel
. . . A ravishing blonde her stockings like a swoon
Asked you something complicated, possibly very pleasant, but
you didn't understand

You had just come from the depths of Moldova and a few
evenings ago
You had sat down to dinner with your mother, father and sisters
Here the pallid mirrors multiplied you, it was warm, you sensed
autumn's approach outside
Like a disappointment dispatched from the depths of Moldova
with its usual winds
With its old rain, with the old familiar water leaking from
the sky onto pavement.
Outside again, everything colder, darker, more desolate,
Raindrops falling idly while your blood roamed same as always
through the flesh of unsaid words
Always the same, the pleasure of the blonde girl buried in your skin
Like a ten-thousand-year-old echo, like a sealed grave
Absurd, high, superb, that bestial souvenir in the rain
In your clothes, in your hair, in your brain, the entire hotel room
The scent of warm skin and brothel silk, it was Paris Paris pale light
Shuttered inside the room and in that light alone but still alive
Embraced by strange arms, by midnight hands that
Quelled your tempest and your blood with rag-soft caresses
It was Paris Paris you fell asleep late, O! To sink into pillows
In your home sleep, in your true sleep, in your waxen sleep.
. . . .
And only in the morning, when swords of brilliant sunlight
Stormed through the window and pierced the mirror
With the reek of gasoline and the noise of engines and footsteps
on the street
Only then did your soul, sniffing the light, brighten a little
And you took it out in the fresh air like a dog, walking
untrod streets
In the clear white morning light of Paris.

[FOR AN INSTANT]

for an instant. for a single instant the world stops existing and rewinds like a film played from the end to the beginning. chimneys inhale their smoke. heights collapse. my footsteps drag me backwards. the glances we cast reverse like the fingers of a glove turned inside out. the core of fruit simplifies flattens spreads into petals. fruit turns to flower. my heart descends into foetal night and transforms into sex.

DIURNAL MOMENT

The road meets a shack
the shack turns green (it was always green)
lemonade fizzes in cold metal strips
I grab a glass and do imaginary things
walk down to the beach and see a girl resembling a boat
and pretending not to know what a woman is
I ask the bathing girl
"Who sliced your belly, between your thighs, like a melon?"
no-one, she says, that's where love is made,
bizarre,
I just stand in the shack and gaze at the nickel-plated machinery.

FUGUE

More than twenty petrified women, grow in a garden
like marble orchids,
a little pale, cadaverous,
wildflowers braiding with their thighs,
and the wild red poppy sleeps its silk on the curly sex
and after death,
the fugue in sharp I,
on the lacy tips of plants,
on a tranquil, boring, sunny afternoon
I, only I, know the miracle of these ivory stones,
death life sculptures
where blood has stopped (a withered tree)
in a hidden body, like ribbons in opaque boxes.

SHORT PROSE

It was from Herrant that I first heard the story of the green ray. He had been told it by his life drawing teacher, but said that he had had his own suspicions long before, without knowing anything for certain. Apparently, the grain of salt the priest had placed on his tongue a few days after he was born was green and strangely luminous. And he was sure, for his memory was excellent — and besides, nothing else could have caused it, as he had only just been born — that this grain of salt had altered the cells of his tongue and imprinted green rays onto it.

At the age of seventeen, when he found out about the ray, the saltiness surged in his taste buds and delivered its clear message.

We lay together in the carriage, on the pier, waiting for the green ray.

The sun turned red, then redder and redder. Then flattened.

And then suddenly, the green ray shot through a white cloud, swift and self-assured, all the way to the edge of the sky. It was such an intense, such a true green that it might have escaped from the vellum pages of our Physics textbook.

"Herrant," I cried, "Herrant, the green ray!"

Silence.

"Herrant!"

I looked at him in the mirror. The Egyptian was asleep. It was pointless to wake him. The green ray was already on its way to another Herrant who had doubtlessly been waiting for it through eight years of illness, urging it that very moment to grant him his most precious wish.

Herrant would have cried — proclaiming his single thought, single wish :

"I want to rise, I want to walk."

We will return tomorrow and wait for his ray.

Berck-Plage

DON JAZZ

I never knew his real name. Don Jazz was evidently a nickname.

Don Jazz was a tall, swarthy Spaniard that used to regale us in the dining hall with stories about the music halls of Paris and other extraordinary things, or show off the latest handkerchief he had purchased : *Très bon marché, n'est-ce pas?*

The first time we met he told us all about Buenos Aires, where he had practised law. Most of the things he described we already knew from novels :

"You know, in Buenos Aires . . . the women . . . you understand . . . they have waiting rooms for their clients . . . you get my meaning . . . just like doctors or dentists. The Madam . . . well, you know what I mean . . . comes downstairs from time to time to ask who's next in line . . ."

This was pure Albert Londres.

The first thing that struck me about this Don Jazz was this profusion of "you know what I mean," this improbable coyness so at odds with his massive, overindulged animal body, like a flower planted in a barrel, and then all the other contradictions between his physical and psychological elements.

(His cough, for instance, contrasted with his sneezing. It was a serious cough, full of conviction and savoir-faire, the cough of a sensible man. His sneezing, on the other hand, was childish, comic and inconsonant.)

But it was more than that. His very organs seem to contradict or wage war on each other.

If our Spaniard had not been moulded from a single piece,

his various organs would have committed a series of intimate assassinations. It feels almost superfluous to add that his gestures did not match his speech. I remember, for instance, one time when he declared that he couldn't stand checked socks : he bowed his head as if cowered by a swift and powerful blow, then nervously opened his hand and stretched out his fingers, his whole body twisted into a question mark.

"They're just a craze . . . it's very strange . . . don't you think? . . . a craze . . ."

Judging by his gestures, checked socks belonged to the mysterious realm of metaphysical forces that dictated the way we live our lives or floss our teeth. In other words, they were directly related or equivalent to Sky, Storms, Transparence, Cells, and Arsenic.

But the way he spoke, as you can see, was understated.

The gestures were pillars while the words were prayers, or vice versa.

Don Jazz died as a result of a geometrical dissension, which, of course, was mostly his doing.

This is what happened : his brain was weaving a thought towards the moon, a sharp thought, vertical and fine, because, as everyone knows, the moon is high above, and not around us, otherwise it wouldn't be a moon, but a kind of earthquake.

His hand, however, weaved a horizontal thought which, unfortunately, he illustrated using a revolver. The bullet then passed through one temple to the other in a horizontal line and when it intersected the vertical thought, Don Jazz died.

The doctors failed to untangle this muddle of perpendiculars.

Berck-Plage, August 1929

LIMITS

aphorisms

I

As we all know, the principles of theft and property are the same.

The process is different, but it is settled by mutual agreement, something we tend to ignore.

The proletariat's goal is to transform into the bourgeoisie.

II

I hate the amiability some people show us only because once upon a time we helped them out of a mess.

The scale of stupidity passes through all heads; it is diminished by glares.

The instinct of self-preservation is the purest, yet most aggressive form of stupidity.

The scientist's idealism relies on a faith in necessary untruths. It justifies their ego and social standing.

A scientist : a calculator of illusions.

III

If we were to be entirely logical, we would go back to sleep the moment we awoke.

The arriviste's modesty is his greatest indulgence.

Hubris, more human than life itself.

IV

The imperfection we chisel at as we evolve, day after day, is more necessary than dangerous.

Those who fascinate us most are those who listen to us : our answers are shaped by how we imagine they see us, rather than how we see them.

Everyone's attention is directed towards "the other." In this way, everyone lives in a reciprocity that belongs to no-one.

In love, we never rediscover ourselves, because what we are seeking has been stolen by the other. This is what we find.

It is a common fallacy to see logic as metaphysical.

Paradoxically, generalisations seem more valid when their subject matter is multifaceted. In such cases, we can easily find examples to support them.

Being original doesn't make you free.

We often console ourselves by ignoring the mediocrity of a deed and imagining it as unique. For the first time in the history of ideas, originality has become "an aim in itself."

Note to the anxious : the ability to conceptualise one's existence and the ability to live unthinkingly are not binary concepts, therefore they cannot cancel each other out. Entry into the world of mind or existence is watched over by absolutely harmless meanings.

Each of us needs an alternative universe : a universe of myth.

People are driven insane because once they have done something insane they lose the taste for wisdom.

If women didn't prostitute themselves, money would soon lose its value in social life.

When some people apologise for a mistake, they convince themselves that you owe them something.

Beauty is destined to disappear, because it can only be bred from regret. The enthusiasm it generates sustains our very being : *we* ourselves, *considering beauty* — and this argument is clearly understood by "art lovers," which must appall them.

Everyone insists on their sincerity, as if it were possible to be insincere for even a second.

People do not commit suicide; when they are driven to this act, it can only be considered an assassination.

Berck-Plage

BUȚU

Wherever people group together under the rigour of a common discipline, a society immediately establishes itself as a hierarchy flanked by two well defined personalities : the chief and the scapegoat.

On the veranda of our sanatorium, Monciu is the chief and Buțu is the scapegoat.

All day long, the conflict between these two simmers with intensity, and even at night the "chief" swears at the "scapegoat" and threatens him in his sleep.

While Monciu shouts, Buțu stays silent.

In our society, Buțu plays the role of the convenient victim : "Buțu, stop making so much noise! Buțu, don't stain the covers! Buțu turned off the light! What are you doing, man? Buțu turned on the light! What are you doing, man, I nearly bumped into you!"

Buțu remains imperturbably calm and retreats into his interior life. He is withdrawn, his smile at once enigmatic and terribly sad.

"Monciu, please give me back my book."

"What book, man?"

"My book, the one you took from me."

"I don't have it, it's on the table," comes the logical reply.

"Well, go get it," (just as logical) "and give it to me."

"What am I, your postman?"

"OK, then, please make sure that the orderly doesn't put a plate of food on it."

"What am I, your servant?"

"Monciu, give me back my book!"

"What do you want, man? Why do you keep bugging me? Are you giving me orders? What are you, man? My sovereign? King? Emperor?"

Monciu's eyes glint with fury and his fists clench, ready for attack. Buțu lowers his eyes and stays silent : he knows he's not a sovereign (nor a king, nor an emperor).

He has one consolation that gets him through these tribulations : the manageress. But even her tenderness is stained with the bitter juice of reproach. It is true that every quarter of an hour Buțu might be granted a crumb of kindness, but just as true that in the next quarter of an hour he's likely to be slapped.

Buțu neither rebels, nor is he resigned.

The mission of his adult life is clear and definite : he will be responsible for everything in life.

JENICĂ

My neighbour, in the bed on my left, is a poet from Oltenia. Under his pillow he hides a penknife and a notebook full of verses. The doctor has promised him that on his twelfth birthday he will lift him out of bed and take him for a walk. Jenică has carefully noted the date in his diary and, immobilised in plaster, like a baby bird clutched in a fist, waits . . .

. . . His head is slightly bowed, leaning on his hand, and he stares at the sea, frowning. He knows the exact number of ships that sail from Constanța every day and which ones are bound for Constantinople; he recognises "that American one that puffs out steam from all the chimneys" and expertly informs all his neighbours when a warship sails past — which he can identify by the cannons and turrets as either a torpedo boat, a destroyer, or gunboat.

"Would you ever like to go to sea, Jenică?"

"Well, sure, obviously . . ."

"On an American ship?"

"No, on my own, like Alain Gerbault."

"What do you mean?"

"Like Alain Gerbault."

"How do you know about that?"

"From the papers."

It was from the papers, too, that he had learned of the revolution in Havana and that a radio station had been built on the island of Majorca. He had the exotic curiosity of an aesthete : he was only interested in events that took place on distant islands with beautiful names.

He once asked me whether there was a sanatorium for spinal tuberculosis on the island of Haiti and, if not, "where do the Papuan children go?"

The question had a clear subtext; Jenică would have gladly given up the penknife under his pillow to anyone who could have presented him with a tiny Papuan with an apron, curly hairy, and golden nose ring as his new neighbour.

He only trusted me to look at his poetry notebook after we became tight friends, but even then "in secret" and only after extracting the promise that I wouldn't tell anyone what he had written, "no-one at all, not even the wind."

I won't transcribe here Jenică's poetry; it's a "secret," but I can tell you that its subject matter was simple, colourful, fragrant. Jenică describes the sky, the sea, snowdrops.

The poet's intimate response to the fragile flower is expressed purely and earnestly :

"It is a joy to see"

and his reflections on the maritime landscape border on the obvious :

"The sea is still and calm
And clouds hang in the blue realm."

But the notebook also showed signs of some disturbing modernist tendencies. Jenică was a Dadaist without knowing it : his Dadaism was drawn from the subtle, wondrous diversity of dreams. One of his hallucinatory tales was entitled : "The blue horse and the Swiss transatlantic."

I will quote here only the episode of their encounter :

"The horse was driving a motorboat, but realising that it was too slow, he jumped out and galloped on the surface of the water, then bit into the ship's mast so that its propeller remained in his mouth."

And then the miracle :

"When he looked down, he saw his four legs, tail and two wings and realised he could now fly on his own through the air."

Not even the prophet Ezekiel had been granted a more beautiful vision!

But that's all I'm going to tell you about it. Every day Jenică writes a page of his masterpiece, and as soon as the editors hear about it, they will fall over themselves to publish it, offering him riches and glory.

Jenică has no use for either of these, all he needs is rest and sea air. He must get well so that he can sail to Polynesia, alone on a ship with enormous sails.

IX — MIX — FIX

for Marie, an acrobatic entertainment

I

Our daily bread is kneaded out of letters, not flour. Every loaf contains an entire Zola novel. On the surface of a crumb, I read a spine-tingling episode involving a catastrophe on the railways.

The count partakes of the same bread, only he prefers it in thin, dare I say almost anonymous, slices.

The soles of his feet are painted red (his feet are bare even though his legs are respectably clad in hunting trousers), he wears a cap decorated with postcards from Brazil, and in his hand he holds a terrifying black lily.

The count likes to boast that he never forms any intimate bonds with anyone.

"I look down on everybody, and never from a height of less than 34 metres."

"Thirty-three in the case of domestic staff," I suggested.

"Never. They throw me up cups of coffee as I fly high above them. I can't lower my standards, both my parents were counts."*

While we were talking, the acrobats had unrolled the bars from their sheaths and were setting up a trapeze on the pavement. Through my soap-smeared window, the street looked as if it were engulfed in fog, even more futile than usual. In the gloom, the uncanny, faded glint of the nickel trapeze bars transformed them into silver fish swimming in a bowl of murky water.

* Evidently impossible, so clearly the count was an impostor.

II

I flew through chaotic chambers walled by bulbous, diseased clouds. I was hanging by the belly of a flying half-dog, my fingers digging into its flesh. But my legs were too long and, as they manically raced on the metal floor, metre-high sparks burst under my feet. Solitude chased me, flying towards me with a keener, sharper melancholy : I could no longer tell whether the rush of speed raced through my body or my soul.

The dog's belly began to melt into the calf of a marble woman, then the cold stone softened into warm, perfumed humanity, into a smooth stocking embroidered with ferns and lion heads.

III

In front of my bed, the parrot theatre has ended its first performance with a quarrel. I would like to stretch out my foot and stroke them, but the room is filled with water, and I lie at its edge, a block of old wood fringed with a lace of decay.

The poet — tall, erect, dark — emerges from the wings and opens his cape to show me a red silk fan pinned to his chest.

Meanwhile, the dining room table suddenly stretches its legs.

I turn my head.

Those four thin wooden columns begin to climb towards the ceiling. A blue ribbon is hanging between them, suspended by a spider's thread, the ribbon of a schoolgirl, leisurely swaying, as if alerting me, with deranged precision, to its irreality.

INSINUATIONS

aphorisms

In general, the law pays little attention to justifications, because they make all deeds seem equal. When it comes to justifications, there isn't much difference between committing a crime and buying a bouquet of flowers : there are the same amount of logical, human reasons why one might choose to do either.

In order to function effectively, justice must necessarily be illogical and inhuman.

In other words, unjust.

Plausibility feels truer than truth. It might be worth investigating, in fact, whether we actually live in a plausible world, rather than a real one.

Philosophy begins with a certain mystification of our understanding, just as beauty begins with a certain mystification of reality.

Whenever we discuss anything with anyone, we are primarily conversing with our own ego, often with a person somewhere far away and only sometimes with the person present.

A bomb can destroy the factory that created it.

This fable is entitled "The Struggle Between Generations."

Some people make others miserable by oppressing them, while others, conversely, by supporting them.

The punishment for hypocritical actions is that they end up being committed in earnest.

There will always be someone who, when a room is silent, will declare something idiotic in a loud voice.
It is the magnetism of the abyss that looms over every conversation.

BERCK, KINGDOM OF THE DAMNED

reportage

On the Paris-Boulogne line, there is a station where all the trains stop for a minute longer than usual. It is Rang-du-Fliers, the connecting station for Berck. When arriving here, the unsuspecting ordinary traveller, rubbing his sleepy eyes while gazing casually out of the train window, will momentarily imagine that he has drifted into a nightmare.

While in all other stations he would have encountered the ordinary babel of travellers hurriedly embarking and disembarking from the train, here he will see orderlies and porters hauling stretchers heavy with moribund patients out of the carriages with infinite care. Cripples hobble on crutches and bodies ravaged by rickets cling desperately to the arms of their companions. They are here on a pilgrimage to Berck, the sanatorium town, the most astounding town in the world, the Mecca of spinal tuberculosis.

This entire crowd will be squeezed into a train as tiny as a toy, with a locomotive that resembles a camel and sluggishly pulls out, noisily puffing and spewing too much smoke — far too much smoke given that it only travels five kilometres. It is the famous "tortillard," the little Berck train filled with Berck's patients and their relatives.

Naturally, the only topic of conversation on this train is illness, patients, cures and treatments. I believe there is more discussion of sickness on this little train than in all the Academies of Medicine in the world put together.

On the other hand, the traveller who has previously been

informed that Berck is the destination of five thousand patients immobilised in plaster will be primed from the very start of the journey for revelatory signs of its singular melancholic character. Upon disembarking, he will be bewildered to find only a banal little provincial town with an Avenue de Gare identical to any other that can be found in every little provincial French town, with a banal high street, with ordinary people idly shopping, with old-fashioned houses reeking of mould and stale air.

Yet Berck's true character will be suddenly revealed to this traveller the moment he turns a street corner and is faced with the first patient lying in a carriage. The vision is stupefying.

Imagine a kind of rectangular pram with a swing at the back, a kind of crate, a kind of boat on wheels conveying a sick person, swaddled in blankets, steering a horse. You're probably imagining someone lying back in a carriage in a comfortable and fairly normal position. No. The patient is completely supine in the wooden frame, gazing upwards, into the void. He does not turn his head to the right, to the left, doesn't lift it, cannot move it : his eyes stare into a mirror affixed above him to a brace that can be shifted in different directions. The carriage passes, turns a corner, avoids a child, stops in front of a shop and all the while the driver's eyes are lost in the ether while his hands pull the reins this way and that, with the gestures of a blind man groping his way through darkness. There is something sad and surreal in this stare, something that indeed resembles the faltering journey of the blind, their sticks feverishly tattooing the pavement as their milky eyes gaze out with indefinable vagueness.

The patient in the carriage is impeccably dressed, with an open jacket, tie, white pocket square, gloves. Who would ever guess that underneath his shirt he is encased in plaster, a white, rigid armour, which he just might be able to shed in three months' time?

A NOTE ON PLASTER

. . . because Berck is the kingdom of immobility and plaster. All the broken, decayed bones from every corner of the world gather here so that they might be straightened and mended. Deformed, crooked spines, loose joints, rotten vertebrae, misshapen elbows, crooked fingers, crooked legs, all gather here praying for the miracle of plaster. Plaster defines Berck just as steel defines Creuzot — it is Liverpool's coal, Baku's oil.

Some plaster casts encase only fingers and others encase entire bodies. Some plaster casts are like aqueducts from which the patient can escape whenever he wants and others, the most terrible of all, are hermetically sealed for entire months. Aside from the torture suffered while the plaster is drying, during which the patient feels as if he is lying in a cold, oppressive swamp, he must also endure the torment of not being able to wash for several months. Naturally, during this time a thick layer of dirt accumulates on the skin, becoming infernally itchy and sore. These types of casts are becoming increasingly rare nowadays.

A HORIZONTAL TOWN

At the first bookshop you come across in Berck, you can buy a guidebook explaining that the town occupies a privileged position on the English Channel as the bay of Authie directs favourable ocean currents towards it.

The same guidebook will inform you that the air in Berck is

incredibly clean, extraordinarily pure, in fact the purest air in the world, with only four bacteria per cubic metre, while in Paris the same volume would contain nine hundred thousand bacteria. For the ailing visitors who have travelled here in the hope of restoring their health and who know they are likely to spend several years in Berck, these are not insignificant indices.

But I can confirm that not one of the five thousand invalids in Berck have been attracted to come here by these boasts of ocean currents and clean air. There is another reason why they flock to this place : it is because in Berck the sick, the disabled, the paralysed, all those disinherited by life, who in other towns lived as pariahs, hidden by their families, shut away in stuffy rooms, profoundly humiliated by the life that defiantly thrives all around them, can regain some normalcy.

The entire town is organised in such a way that they can live a perfectly ordinary life even as they permanently lie horizontal and undergo treatment. Horizontal, they can "go" to the cinema, take carriage rides, go to a nightclub, attend a conference, or visit each other. Their gurneys can pass through every door in Berck, enter any public place, any shop : in Berck, not one of the buildings has a doorstep. Life has been reorganised here by rotating 90 degrees, proving that a horizontal existence is perfectly feasible.

In the grand hotels, sick men and women reside in rooms no different to any other hotel room and take their meals in dining rooms specially designed to accommodate them, where they are wheeled to their tables on gurneys. The spectacle of these dining rooms is simultaneously strange and sumptuous. Sumptuous because it resembles a Roman banquet where all the guests recline on their backs, but strange because the sickly pallor of these revellers brings to mind some kind of hallucinatory tale by Edgar Allan Poe.

But even more surprising is the spectacle of the beach during the summer months, where the patients flirt with the beautiful women who flock around them. And these flirtations are not always innocent. I have already mentioned that the sick come to Berck to become normal again . . .

Of course there is also drama, and unbearable heartbreak. But in Berck, the consequences are seldom tragic. Last winter, a hysterical woman and her incurably ill lover committed suicide under a calvary cross. The incident caused a stir, and Parisian reporters spun some wonderfully embellished tales about the tragic town of Berck. In truth, though, such cases are the exceptions.

Caught up in the rhythm of an almost ordinary life, the sick wear their misery lightly.

This is the psychological miracle of Berck.

WHAT IS A GURNEY?

For the sick, the carriage drives are a real blessing.

But it is an expensive, extravagant blessing. Patients in Berck might pay between twenty-five and thirty francs for a couple of hours' carriage rental. To their frustration, the town council has never stepped in to regulate the price of locomotion. So patients pay almost fifteen lei for a fifteen minute ride, about as much as it would cost to run the engine of a luxury car for the same time. Because at Berck, you see, a horse drawn carriage is the equivalent of a Rolls-Royce.

Under these circumstances, the health benefits of the sea air and the pleasures of outings would be enjoyed only by the privileged few were it not for the gurney, a mode of transportation that is universally available. The gurney is an invention that transforms a sick person into a healthy one. It combines the functions of a bed, a carriage, and a healthy pair of legs into one. A gurney is a stretcher with four large rubber wheels, a frame that supports the supine body of the patient and tough springs that prevent it from juddering on bumpy roads.

In the cheaper sanatoria, where patients of slender means lie side by side in communal wards, the gurneys are only used for seaside promenades. But in certain hotels and guesthouses, the patients are permanently installed on their gurneys. They sleep on them, eat on them, lie on them during outings. Patients can navigate their whole room on a gurney, simply by dropping their arms and manoeuvring its wheels in any direction. For example, I have seen an invalid "walking" in this way to his bookcase to get a book or independently cruising the corridors.

A patient who wants to buy something in town will immediately telephone a nearby sanatorium and a former patient or convalescent will be employed to push his gurney to the chosen destination.

The fee for this service is five lei. In Berck, a human being is cheaper than a horse and just as serviceable.

HOTELS AND SANATORIA

The brochure advertising Berck explicitly claims : "Berck offers treatment facilities that cater to all patients, regardless of their financial situation." This is perfectly true. The difference, however, between an "up-to-date"* hotel and a "budget" sanatorium

* English in the original. [Tr.]

is as vast as that between a distinguished gentleman dressed in a tailored ash-grey suit with a boutonnière and the beggar in rags who stretches his hand towards him in supplication.

All of the grand hotels in Berck promise green lawns fringed with splendid flowers, elevators and running water. All of the "budget" sanatoria have dank walls, smelly corridors and dirty floors. The difference between the clinical treatments and general morale in these places corresponds to their outward appearance. Even so, there are a couple of notable exceptions — two Berck hospitals catering to the poor, both of them admirably organised along the principles of common decency. They are the Maritime Hospital, belonging to the Public Assistance Institution of Paris, and the Franco-American Hospital, a charitable institution. The trouble is that the former only admits Parisian patients while the latter has very few spaces available. A patient in reduced circumstances who cannot find a place at either of these institutions thus falls prey to the entrepreneurial operators of the "budget" sanatoria.

BERCK, KINGDOM OF THE DAMNED

In Berck, five thousand spinal tuberculosis patients lie immobilised in plaster, waiting to be healed. The dreadful illness discerningly targets the joints — the vertebrae, hips, knees — and the attacked area must be immobilised immediately. Five thousand patients lie on gurneys and beds, lost in their reveries, endlessly absorbed in their endless books, dematerialised by their infinite contemplation of the ocean's immensity.

Healing is slow, unbearably slow, but it does happen. Nowadays, we see miracles that no-one could have ever dreamed of in the past. Over Berck's fifty year history, a rational approach and constantly improving therapeutics have reduced the mortality rates for bone tuberculosis from 80% in the last century to 5% at present, a unique achievement in the annals of medicine.

What's more, in Berck the patients live a normal life and the horrendous curse of their physical limitations becomes more bearable in the midst of a community filled with others like them.

But one cannot help but be moved by Berck. From the drama of the sick being hoisted onto carriages like coffins onto hearses (just like hearses, the carriages have rollers to help the patient slide into them), to the spectacle of perspiring patients knitting in the sun and peddling their creations for a few coins to holidaymakers, Berck is filled with striking, heart-rending scenes.

Yet I have never seen anything so moving, so profoundly human and sad as the Christmas liturgy at Berck. The Catholics celebrate the birth of Christ in church at midnight. Nothing can be more affecting than the extraordinary emotion of the sick, their ecstatic pallor, during the quiet solemnity of the Midnight Mass.

Scattered amongst the crowd, mothers and relatives are seen stifling their desperate sobs into handkerchiefs while the priest weaves between the ailing with the Eucharist — every diseased body suddenly transfigured, trembling as it receives divine grace.

During the moment of "elevation," when all the faithful sink to their knees, the patients simply cover their eyes with their hands. At that moment the silence in the church deepens, swells, while outside the rain pummels the staves and the wind hollers its sinister chant as if beckoning all the world's damned with its all-encompassing, ravaging wail.

FEVER

(from the notebook of Arthur Hogg)

The room smells of vetiver, toothpaste and eau de cologne. The electric light is as stale as sun-faded newspapers. On a chair in the middle of the room, where a wounded man languishes, a nurse is dozing, her eyes fixed on the floor as if keeping vigil by the window of a panopticon.

Outside, birdsong pierces the rustle of waves.

Thoughts blend into each other and cannot coagulate into any desire, epiphany or phrase. Life's meaning reduces itself to an ample vibration that filters — from where? — into this hermetic, ashen portion of air.

A tooth sprouts from every bone, and from every tooth, a plant. The plants fall to the floor, discussing their predicament.

Chasms open afresh.

MAB
(from the notebook of Arthur Hogg)

The sun has set. On the esplanade, the gas lamps wait to be lit. Wide, quiet shreds of clouds rise from the sea. Mab watches them through the window.

"Look, three horsemen! What a sad country they roam! Now, look, a procession. See there, in the middle, a pale, naked courtesan lying in a carriage. A bronzed boy plays a pipe behind it, counting his steps."

He watches the clouds unravelling.

•

The lights on the esplanade flicker awake. The sky grows darker and darker. Silence purrs above the waves, floating above the roar of the world as it battles against a burden of water at the bottom of the ocean. It is the silence of a shell's emptiness, of watch repair shops, of pillows and herbs.

•

Sitting in silence together, Mab and I, the words we want to say to each other seem to belong to other people, living somewhere far away. Perhaps that's why we listen so intently.

•

Everything around us is too heavy, too immutable. The books

are fixed on the shelves in a senseless order, a stain of light on a vase of flowers glares at the window and the curtains sway slowly, so slowly that it seems they will never be still.

•

There is also a cat in the room. "A cat," Mab says, "is pure animal, because, you see, she moves, moves, moves and maybe a thought enters her head. If it does, worse luck for her."

•

Everything is too immutable and this nothingness that surrounds us strains to contain the entirety of life.

Aside from that, I'm almost certain we are alive.

"Isn't that so, Mab? We're alive?"

"Ah, you, and your morbid curiosity!," Mab exclaimed. "For nosy people like you life should begin on the other side of death. Then, you would have all the time in the world to dissect it at your leisure and stop chasing after it."

•

Someone has turned on the light in the room. A different Mab, different flowers, a different cat. Time stirs awake this evening. Evening : a day has passed. What do people do in a day?

•

In a minute, a nurse will come to take me back to my room.

Now I am here, soon I will be there. Everywhere I'll be met with silence and stillness. I would like to have something to look forward to in my life.

•

"Mab, I would like to have something to look forward to in my life."

"Try not to look forward to anything," Mab replied. "You will be richly rewarded : nothing will ever happen."

LOVE

(from the notebook of Arthur Hogg)

. . . you can find plenty of silly justifications to support a good argument. Put simply, I have never been in love. But while I knew this right from the start, she only realised it much too late. There was no way she could understand : I *constructed* our love patiently, with no hesitation, so that *it really might have been* what it pretended to be. I always had a ready answer to her questions and never disturbed the awkward intimacy that haloes every meeting between lovers. The strange thing is that sometimes I had the impression she felt the same way. I mean, if I were to try to pin down this impression I would realise that I never thought of her as I thought of myself, so questioning myself would have been useless as the invariably indifferent response (for me) would have just been her rapt attention. But wasn't I just as attentive?

She would always come to me in the evening. I have always loved the minutes when the sun sets : the mind is at peace and ideas cannot be moulded into words. Lying in bed, I would watch the sunbeams shifting on the ceiling or the faint stain of a cloud at the edge of the window. Books mounted in dead piles beside me. During such moments, books become nothing more than ordinary objects.

I would hear her footsteps down the corridor and cry out "Come in!" without waiting for her to knock. She liked that : the fact that I recognised her steps. But I only called out because I knew that her presence was inevitable. How could she have guessed my reluctance since I never confessed it?

The moment she walked through the door my eyes clung insatiably to the corner of the sky and I was too ashamed to turn my head. If I could have carved out my fate in that moment, I would have chosen to fix it in that blue, my soft bed, my tranquil gaze.

But I had to turn my head. And then I looked at her like I looked at the sky . . .

We were both silent. She sat on a chair with an awkwardness that irritates me even now, as if to say :

"You see, I'm sitting on the chair. I've got to busy myself with something else when all I want to do is look after you. But it's you I always think about."

These words insinuated themselves clearly, especially when she sat beside me on the bed. Then she smiled and her smile said :

"I've put everything aside to come to see you. Now all I have to do is sit here and admire you."

But that wasn't what embarrassed me. As I said : I looked at her like I looked at the sky. But then I had to kiss her. I had to take her hand and intertwine my fingers with hers, noticing their every inflection (as if each were a perfect mirror of our souls, different in form).

But I — if it is possible to say that I existed somewhere outside the confined space of this world reduced to fingers, human forms, a window frame — was in my own world. I was alone and incredibly bored. There was no other way I could feel. Any conversation would have concluded with her still admiring me. She would have said that I was just conjuring a fantasy whose key only I (only He) possessed, thus justifying her complete lack of curiosity. But then, thinking about it rationally, I could not say that I didn't love her. I held her beside me, undressed her, and we reached the same intimacy as the day before, and the one before that, following the same script as always.

Afterwards, we were silent and my mind invariably wandered towards the same conclusion : it is always simpler to accept reality than pursue the things we truly desire.

A solution simultaneously simpler and more dreadful.

If morality were not connected to the actions of real people, then sin and punishment would be fused. What was my sin? What was my punishment? Is my life simply a metaphysical symbol?

I can only answer all these questions with the same eternal indifferences. This is why I feel, *on a human level,* I am guilty. A purely intellectual penitence . . .

Reading these lines, *she,* who might have understood that the only reason I was calm was because excess bored me, would have said to me :

"Be quiet, your entire self is an invention. I feel sorry for you. Why won't you listen to me? Put your head next to me and lie here in peace."

Or :

"Since the soul is always learning, why not find some use for it?"

Of course the soul is constantly learning and of course we could invent a use for it; the usefulness of a clock that can function without hands. A sentimental use. Sentiments, unfortunately, must be named.

And then, if I reject any purpose, it's because I have devoted my entire life to searching for it.

Look at the last phrase I just wrote. False, false, I can *churn* it out at any time, subtly *tweaking* anything that doesn't please me.

I mustn't fool myself. The only reason I analyse my guilt is because I'm trying to reveal the existence of morality. Logic is an admirable form of mental distraction.

I'm only surprised that so far my organs have not become abstractions and their functions have not transformed into ideas.

When that happens, I imagine my love will no longer hold any mysteries for me.

The little square seemed lost in the town, like a white, immaculate page stuck between some yellowing notes in an ancient file. It was a new, clean asphalt patch surrounded by black, ugly houses. The square was a few blocks away from the town hall and when the sweepers started work in the morning, they always made sure it was left impeccably clean. One after another they came, and even if the square had already been swept two minutes earlier, none of them could resist gliding their broom over it one more time, just like children who keep taking out a brass button from their pocket, blowing on it and polishing it on their coats, then again blowing on it, rubbing it on their coat, again looking at it, polishing it . . .

I used to love playing with my friends in that square. Our marbles rolled on the smooth asphalt with satisfying accuracy; it was the place where we played our most special games : marbles, buttons and boardgames, not rough games like stick fighting. This was also the place where we played "French Cavalry," where the boys rode each other like horses, wearing their caps backwards, for some unfathomable reason.

We could always run amok there, without fear of being scolded. Far from it, some people in the neighbourhood liked childish games as much as we did : Ioniță Cubiță for one.

His bakery was right on the edge of the square and even though its sign clearly stated "Ion Cubiță Bakery" everyone called him Ioniță Cubiță, probably due to that anonymous, eternal weakness for prosody that resides in the heart of the masses ("he won't do it, but give him another coin and he'll see to it").

He was short and fat, his face smooth except for a few stray blond hairs on his chin that looked so insubstantial they might have been grown under a hothouse lamp and later glued to his face. He wore some extremely distinguished thin rimmed glasses with golden frames, the most distinguished spectacles in town. The rest of his appearance formed a stark contrast to those glasses : his fingers were full of rings, a thick chain lay on his vest, he spent the whole day either inside his shop or, if he wanted some air, sitting on a chair outside to sell his wares.

His favourite and most diverting pastime was stopping boys on their way home from school and punching them in the Adam's apple, causing the child to feel a sharp pain and a hollowness in the chest . . .

Ioniță Cubiță had another serious hobby : catching stray dogs and stuffing tobacco up their noses.

He would get the dog to come up to him, stroke its head gently, scratch behind its ears, then carefully slide his hand towards its nose and push green tobacco inside the nostrils. The dog would immediately run away, sneezing terribly and chasing its tail as if demented, howling with pain.

All of these things happened in the square, as if it had been a stage built for this purpose; we children would crowd around, laughing, to curry favour with Ioniță Cubiță, who didn't seem to object at all to his popularity.

One day he really shocked us, and the event haunted the tormented dreams of all the children who witnessed it.

Ioniță Cubiță had caught a rat in a trap and presented it to us in the middle of the square. Everyone gathered round, hoping for some first-rate entertainment. And Ioniță Cubiță did seem especially pleased with himself :

“See? Just an ordinary rat, but one that knows how to dance the foxtrot . . . Do you want to see it foxtrot?” he said.

“Yeaaah!,” we shouted in unison.

(And some of the children slowly pronounced, “Foxtrot, foxtrot,” a bizarre, mysterious word they had just heard for the first time.)

Mr. Cubiță laid the trap on the ground and warned us not to touch it. He then went inside the shop and came back out with a gas canister. I can still see him now, walking out of the bakery, waddling on his short, fat legs, holding the canister. He turned on the gas in the direction of the poor animal, took a box of matches out of his pocket and struck one just as he was opening the trap.

The rat, now a smoking ball of flames, darted out, then rolled on the ground, perched on two legs, then jumped around manically.

“Didn’t I tell you, boys, it knows how to foxtrot! Just look how it dances . . . ,” said Ioniță Cubiță, his spectacles dancing gleefully on his nose while his gullet trembled merrily.

Ioniță Cubiță’s fat, damp hands clapped a slow rhythm.

The spectacle of the burning rat and its loud, agonising shrieks were terrifying. At last, its body curled up and transformed itself into a small mound of charred flesh, burning with a pale flame. The stink of burning fat and skin filled the entire little square. The children drew closer and poked at the ashes.

This, then, was Ioniță Cubiță — a short, fat man with blue, slightly bulging eyes staring from behind gold-framed glasses, his fingers covered in rings.

I remember that two or three days after the rat incident an

older boy sent me and another young kid into the bakery to ask Mr. Cubiță if he was planning to set fire to any more rodents.

The other kid went up to the counter and stared straight into the baker's eyes :

"Mr. Antohi sent me to ask you if you've got any more mice to burn."

Ioniță Cubiță pushed the glasses up the bridge of his nose and spoke slowly and deliberately, emphasising every word :

"Get out of here, you motherfucker."

That was Ioniță Cubiță.

One day, Ioniță Cubiță disappeared. Through the ever efficient children's grapevine, we found out that he had liver cancer and that his belly had swollen so much it was likely to burst. For a while he slipped out of our consciousness, and then one day we learned he died.

The blinds of the bakery were now drawn and we could hear a great deal of commotion inside. All of his relatives and acquaintances were gathered within, but we didn't hear a single cry or lamentation. The funeral took place on a summer afternoon. The hearse was led by a procession of trays filled with braided bread as golden and silky as the braids of maidens.

Something unexpected then happened in the cemetery. Before the coffin could be lowered into the grave, the priest demanded that it should be opened. The family wanted him to be buried with the lid closed, but the priest insisted. The sun blazed in the sky. The coffin was opened. He lay there with his sallow face, pathetically scrawny in his wedding suit with silver cufflinks.

And then suddenly, as the priest was sprinkling him with holy water, the rays of sun somehow pierced through the crowd, striking the cadaver, and the dead man's face began to darken, in an instant becoming black as coal.

They quickly shut the lid and lowered him into the ground.

So that was Ioniță Cubiță.

[AIZIC WOLF]

fragments from a notebook

He was always holding a duster, a long, flexible black stick with multicoloured feathers. A cheap, ordinary object he must have bought in some market, but which added a note of elegance to Aizic Wolf's old fashioned suit. Whenever the antiquarian presented an artefact to a customer, he nervously fluttered around it with his feather duster, shifting it to find the most favourable angle as if performing a little minuet, resembling a character you might see in a painting in a museum, except in this case the dancer wore rubber soled shoes instead of satin slippers and brandished a feather duster instead of a beribboned stick.

When Aizic Wolf proposes to Einike, the order of her world changes, as if things suddenly become clear for the first time, like a letter written in invisible ink whose content emerges when a liquid is applied to it.

When Elsa returns to her room, the mundanity of the afternoon strikes her as a revelation, the harbinger of an ending. Until then, her bliss had steadily grown, peaking that morning, on the riverbank.

Guy leaves for Paris, troubled, determined to salvage whatever's left to salvage.

Momentous memories erase themselves like effigies, while "minor" memories grow in significance, fill with details, colour, light.

On the last day of the school term, Elsa visited Aizic Wolf's shop and saw his son return home from college, and now she remembers the light of that first afternoon of holiday and lives inside it for the rest of the day, while the “significance” of today’s events withers.

SELECTED CORRESPONDENCE

Dear Mr. Minet,[1]

I've just been told you telephoned me from Paris to ask if I might have left my map in your carriage, at least that's what the hotel receptionist thought you said. Here's what I think happened : while I was in the carriage, I tucked a regional map inside a book. I can no longer find the map and was in fact searching for it just before you rang, so it must have fallen out and your porter picked it up with the rest of the luggage, and you came across it once in Paris and then decided to phone me so that I wouldn't waste my time looking for it. If this is the case, I can assure you it's not worth your trouble. You can, if you like, put it in an envelope and send it to me when you get the chance. But there is no rush, I have no immediate need for it. Thank you.

It's strange, but your call had a powerful effect on me : the whole time I've been staying in Berck no-one has phoned me from Paris, a fact of little importance in and of itself, but I'm struggling to explain why it somehow concretises my predicament here in Berck (which over the last few days I've felt more and more intensely) of living an immobile existence. I say to myself : so, there is someone in Paris, right at this moment! Talking to me from Paris! Where is he right now? In a café? In a post office? (And I can visualise that café, that post office.) After hanging up the phone you walk out into the street . . .

Of course, one can think about such things at any time, but sometimes a particular event brings them all into relief (because, after all, any number of scenarios might unfold in our minds, but

[1] Pierre Minet (1909-75), avant-garde French poet associated with the para-Surrealist group Le Grand Jeu. He and Blecher met while both were undergoing treatment in Berck-sur-Mer.

in reality our brain focuses only on one thought at a time).

The great sceptic that has made his home inside me right from the start of living in Berck would reply that it's a feeble, superficial philosophy. But being forced by circumstances into scepticism (after all, I'm stuck on a gurney!) at the age of twenty, freshly plucked out of the bosom of my family and my life as a student, is not much fun.

Of course, I am reliably informed that ordinary life is desperately idiotic, but I haven't experienced it for myself!

And even if I had and could attest to its blandness, would that give me reason to stop hating Berck?

But all these words are just rags of logic in which I clothe something you might describe as a life filled more with others than with my own self, full of things that have been abandoned or renounced, a life *I don't understand* (I'm not being humble here and I don't even feel curious about its mysteries. I might even be happy(!) if life truly were a great mystery). So deep down I don't know if it is myself I should hate before I hate Berck.

I will try to immerse myself in work, because it's the only thing that brings me some satisfaction.

And after that? I will keep sinking, I imagine, lower and lower. I probably shouldn't say this, but what is the difference, really, between living in hope and living badly? *I feel* I will keep sinking.

Yours,

M. Blecher

P.S. Excuse the spelling mistakes. I didn't get round to correcting them all, because I wanted to post this letter quickly so you wouldn't worry about the map.

P.P.S. My bookseller sent an order to Éditions du Carrefour.[2] They will give you the copy before they post it. Thank you for the dedication. M.

BERCK, TUESDAY, 21 APRIL 1931

Dear Mr. Minet,

How are you? What did the doctor say? Are you immobilized? I look forward to your reply. I'd like to come to see you, but my carriage is in awful condition. If you are able to walk and *it wouldn't be a bother* to drop by, it would make me very happy to see you.

Yours,

M. Blecher.

P.S. Would you like to borrow some books?

VILLA NORMANDE, BERCK-PLAGE, PAS DE CALAIS, FRANCE, 16 JUNE 1931

Dear Mr. Valerian,[3]

I am sending you a few short pieces that I hope you might be interested in publishing in *Viața literară* [Literary Life]. Some selections have already appeared in *Bilete de papagal* [Parrot Tickets],[4] and in sending these to you now for your consideration I am succumbing to the same old impulses, as clear and self-evident as my hand that is resting its five fingers on these pages . . .

[2] Minet's autobiographical novel *Histoire d'Eugène* (Paris: Éditions du Carrefour, 1930).

[3] Ion Valerian, the pseudonym of Valerie Ionescu (1895-1980), founded in 1926 the bimonthly literary magazine *Viața literară*, serving as its editor. Blecher submitted the three "from the notebook of Arthur Hogg" pieces and the group of aphorisms constituting Part IV of "Limits," but the magazine never published them.

[4] Left-wing satirical daily, and later a weekly literary magazine, edited by Tudor Arghezi. The first to publish Blecher's early prose in 1930 (see Bibliographic Notes).

Besides, I feel the publication of these notebook pieces would give me a sense of equilibrium that would encourage me to continue working on the novel I've been writing for some time, which I think could be valuable in terms of the psychological insight it offers. (Again, vanity probably plays a part in my desire to complete this project.)

Thank you in advance for taking the time to read the enclosed pages.

Respectfully yours,

M. Blecher

P.S. I would be grateful if you would give me your honest opinion.

BERCK, 2 AUGUST 1931

Dear Mr. Minet,

It is impossible for me to comprehend how one manages to write a letter. I stare at the page, at my fingers, completely baffled, no questions run through my mind, nothing comes to light, nothing smells of lavender, nothing lifts me, no "sentiments," no writing paper, no philosophy the colour of of a candelabrum foot, and for all that it still has to be a letter. For you. For Mr. Minet. With an address. With a stamp. *Vivre!!* (Ph. Soupault) *Merde!!* (M. Blecher). Apologies, I mean to say : understand me. As if drawing angels on the surface of a useless sky, should I also add that in the morning at half past seven I thought about your cane, a yellow substance (yes, a substance) always (eternally) flowing from it and sticking to your fingers? (I have told you many times how much I admire your cane. Clearly, this is not the sort of thing one should write about, but I don't care.) Or how much your letter delighted me? Let's not wreck everything — as a matter of principle. One day we will find out what that principle is (it's the price of consumption).

I will tell you a secret, I don't understand it fully myself (what a disagreeable impression), it's about *Le Petit Parisien,*[5] yes, or perhaps about the dining table etc. Let me explain : last month I had an operation. It was very serious. Now I'm better. On 2 July I thought I would die. After that, I don't know what happened (I mean, what happened was that I kept saying to myself over and over again : "I don't know what's happening").

And then one day (the first time anything like this has happened to me), I read *Le Petit Parisien,* I started whistling and told myself that I have to accept I'm alive. *And even now I can't shake that feeling.*

That's all I can manage to write. I grit my teeth, make jokes, stare at the leaves of trees — (I've taken a break from all that *to write to you.* Oh, if it were possible! (an idiotic wish, entirely wrong)).

Accept, dear Mr. Minet, my sincere friendship,

M. Blecher

BERCK, 26 OCTOBER 1931

Dear Mr. Minet,

I know, I know, I know. It's too late. Throw my letters in the fire, along with anything else at hand : a woman, a tree, the Eiffel Tower, burn it all and then write to me that it *all* combusted. When it comes to me, don't be fooled (I can't imagine you would be, although I frequently manage to deceive myself — actually, most of the time) : My thoughts keep turning towards tranquil things, like an orange or a large dictionary. Basically, I'm very,

[5] Popular French newspaper published between 1876 and 1944.

very pleased with myself. Here's one for you : "of course, we have the right to try." We have to try to see *what works*. Of course, if we want to get mystical about it, it's also down to luck . . .

Write to me or tell me to go to hell,

M. Blecher

BERCK, SUNDAY, 17 JANUARY 1932

Dear Minet (to hell with "Mr.," I'm too fond of you),

I'm leaving for Switzerland tomorrow or Tuesday. I have a high fever and have to try to do everything to get better — I like to look after myself, you see. I will pass through Paris and will be there for a total of six hours (from five in the afternoon until eleven in the evening). I would be very glad if you could make it to the station (I will send you a telegram). I hope Switzerland will do me good (I've repeated this phrase to myself so many times over the past few days, without really knowing what it means!).

Come to see me at the station. I won't discuss literature with you, we'll just have a beer together.

See you Monday (Tuesday).

Yours,

M. Blecher

"LES SAPINS," LEYSIN, SWITZERLAND, 14 FEBRUARY 1932

Dear Minet, my dear Minet,

I've been writing long letters to you in my mind every day for a month. In vain I wait for your address as if — will you believe me? — it's the only thing worth waiting for, the thing I long for the most. I've been very depressed. I told one of my friends (an imbecile who understands nothing) : "At the moment the reasons I have for living are the same as the ones I have for dying." Since my so-called recovery, I've stupidly wasted my energy on daily walks or on the intelligent mechanics of life (intelligent life . . . well, you know what it means!) without finding anything of real significance. I have many things to tell you and will try to write them all, because it brings me pleasure.

First of all, about the people, and then about my recovery. The people I've met here are all self-satisfied snobs, full of firm convictions. At the moment I'm reading the letters of Dostoevsky, I reread Oscar Wilde's *De Profundis,* some Verhaeren and other writers who have felt all the things the snobs are *too afraid to feel.* I wonder what's the point of their beautiful revolt and *splendid spiritual honesty.* When I listen to the insipid, trite prattle of a particular gentleman whom I visit (!), and who introduces me to his acquaintances as "Dr. Blecher," meaning to flatter me, I feel as if I'm living in an epoch when the soul has just now made its appearance. Inside us is a "thinking animal" that resembles any other animal. When it comes to everyone I meet here, this animal is at the foetal stage. I don't really care, but it makes life that much harder.

In addition, I'm acquainted with some completely "undistinguished" Englishmen. I like them better (O, God, if I could achieve that state of grace where I could have at least a little understanding of what I do and feel), but they are part of the great hodgepodge of the *"this cannot be"* set. (This is possible, this is not possible.) How ridiculous not to be able to say, "I think the opposite is true" — but it would be childish. There is no hope of salvation here. (Any religious language I use should be understood in the secular sense — not tied to any ideology.)

Just yesterday evening (bear with me, I have a cold and my thoughts are running in all directions!) I told myself to stop all this and try to change. But, my dear Minet, you know better than I of how little worth is this desire to become someone *other*.

And yet, "it's still possible to live!" you say — we constantly tell ourselves this. Fine for you — and for me — but meaningless.

On another topic : my recovery. It was a myth. They got me up on my feet again thinking that it would help me *heal*, not because I have actually healed.

How can I dampen the benevolent enthusiasm of my parents and friends who believe I've recovered? It's their problem. My problem is the one I mentioned above. *I don't want to get to the stage where I'm incapable of making any decisions.* I think I'll be able to change and everything will improve. If my health allows it, starting today I will replace every moment I've lost with a moment gained, starting today I will be less fascinated by everything that is unfascinating. (You've already reached that stage, and I greatly admire you for this.) (I'm sure if I were to confess this to that gentleman — see above — he would reply, "I understand, you've become an ascetic," and if I were to reply that it's not a question of "making my arse thinner or fatter," he would retort, "What is it, then?," and wouldn't find a way to define it. And such a luminous definition seems to appear inside me!)

————————————

A while ago, I started thinking about the notebook I sent you. I think I've discovered its main flaw. There is an imagination that belongs to reality — it concerns those things that need to be expressed. But I express the imagination of the imaginary. It's not a work of art, but a document.

————————————

The sensitive reader blessed with natural intelligence unwittingly intuits something when instead of saying Surrealists are "complete fantasists" says "there's *much more* to life than you think." Of course, the foolish reader will say the opposite, and Surrealists only seem to listen to this type of reader. As a result, their writings become known for eliciting the exclamation : "they are complete fantasists!"

————————————

I have several good ideas at the moment, but if I tell you about them before I put them down on paper (as Dostoevsky says, "white on black, that's all that counts"), I would inevitably spoil them. I would be very happy if I managed to achieve what I intend and to send you a few pages from time to time. I am feverish with excitement at the thought of creating good work. If only I could rid myself of this immense block of laziness weighing on me (to be honest, it doesn't really weigh on me, *I am laziness itself* — or maybe my thoughts have completely deserted me, but this is not possible, so if I start to believe it, I am lost. There are people who possess not a drop of the spirit of the tormented, but who, due to their excessive good health, still believe themselves to be tormented, etc.).

————————————

You tell me about your suffering and your physical aches. I've thought about this, in my own way, and I don't know what to say to you. I have also suffered a great deal and still have unpleasant pains (for example, when pure alcohol is poured on my wounds, etc.). What can I say to you? Dare I ask you, I wonder : "is your suffering red?" or "is your suffering green?" or "is your suffering like a spiral?" or "does your suffering resemble a giraffe?" Like the priests do, to pass the time? (Truly, this is what some consolers do

— because, don't you think, there's a *method to consoling?*) Let's call it bollocks, *much sillier that way.*

—————————————

(But still, my mind comes back to the pain. How hard it must be for you, and how sorry I am that it has to be that way. I can't think of anything to write to you because I can imagine that pain exactly. If I knew a special trick that could make it go away, it would be the *only thing* I would write to you about, but I haven't even found one for myself. The day before yesterday, when my wounds started to burn again, I told myself I should try to find the voluptuousness in it. You know what I'm about to say. I failed. *I couldn't feel happy until the pain subsided.*)

—————————————

(Another parenthesis. I would like to hold on to the image that has just passed through my mind : we are walking together down a street — it doesn't matter which, but it's a sunny day. I don't know what you're saying to me, but you're smiling; your clothes suit you (I can't help it, that's what I'm imagining) and, once again, a beautiful day. Where are we going? *But we have no pain.* It's beaaauuutiful.)

—————————————

I met a fairly intelligent young girl recently (on the street, obviously, not in a salon, where up till now I've never been lucky enough to meet a single interesting person). We had a conversation, but I'm embarrassed to say I wasn't a good listener. I'll tell you more about her in another letter, because it seems to me that her ideas are marred by all the flaws I want to free myself from.

—————————————

Now I am thinking about you and your operation etc. I would really like it to be successful : this instead of a wish. Could the friendship I send you "with all my joy" (for "with all my heart") also substitute for a thing? If I were a piece of iron I would send it to you as iron, but since I'm a human, I send it to you as thoughts. Forgive me for expressing myself in such a literary fashion, all I'm really trying to say is that I care for you.

Yours,

M. Blecher

P.S. I'm posting the letter right away, without rereading it.

P.P.S. Give my regards to Jacqueline when you see her.

P.P.P.S. I remember that when you were in Berck your friends would send you "the latest books," which you would then sell. If you have any more, please give them to Jacqueline and ask her to send them to me, and thank her in advance for me. (I'll write to her too). I'll send them back to you via courier or, if there are any you no longer need, I'll pass them on to others in the sanatorium. The book selection in the library here is too classical and I need a "break" from it now and then. At the moment, I don't have any money to buy books. Thank you.

"LES SAPINS," LEYSIN, SWITZERLAND, 29 FEBRUARY 1932

Dear Minet (done),

The world is very unstable and I'm terrified of everything, an ordinary card game in a Parisian café might cause a ship to sink off Madagascar or, because I'm in Switzerland and feel changed (in essence I'm still *myself, myself, myself,* only without hope), it might be a sign you will not write to me. It's stupid (*on my part*), almost a *contrived* naiveté (isn't it? just like when you're falsely accused you defend yourself less effectively than if the accusation were true, because when you do some misdeed you already have an excuse).

I await, then, a word from you and your new address, of course. When I passed through Paris, I couldn't get hold of you (on the phone). I'll tell you all about it in another letter.

Yours,

M. Blecher

"LES SAPINS," LEYSIN, 20 OCTOBER 1932

Dear Minet,

I'm not sure if you remember the three manuscripts I sent you almost a year ago. If you still happen to have them lying around somewhere, and if you don't mind, please send me the section that starts with "walking down the streets in pursuit of a dream . . ." You can keep the rest, if you like, although they're of no importance. The pages that I would like you to send have a special resonance for me . . . I will write you at greater length. How is your health? I never received a reply to my last letter.

I remain forever yours, sincerely,

M. Blecher

MONDAY, 10 FEBRUARY 1933

Change of address : "La Valerette," Leysin, Switzerland

Dear dear Minet,

Every letter from you brightens me, the pleasure goes to my head and I feel possessed by a beautiful madness at the thought of receiving news from you, in other words, that you truly exist — that you exist — somewhere. Believe me, or don't, but please believe me : your letters are almost the only ones *I look forward to.* In addition — this time — I've been very touched by the message you've sent me from L.P. Quint.[6] I will respond to him myself, without delay before 20 March. It goes without saying that I'm grateful for everything you do for me. I would so love to see you again. Unfortunately, my health is very poor at the moment and it is likely that I will soon be returning to Romania, to a sanatorium on the Black Sea. A trip to France doesn't seem to be on the cards. Ah, if only I felt better, or — the ultimate prize — if I could be cured!

Dear Minet, those last few pages I sent you — I mean the typed ones, not the old manuscripts where I was just beginning to learn what it means to be a writer — yes, those pages seem to me at odds with everything I now feel I could write. It's not a question of being satisfied with them, but rather a feeling of happiness. The things you once wrote about harmony now echo inside me. Yes, I feel their orchestral fluid flowing inside me — I listen to it with my inner ear that receives sounds and is itself a musical organ. I no longer see any difference between the form and content of language, the two merge into one. And yet I'm far from the point where I'm grinning in contentment with a literary gut full of satisfaction ready to be excreted — I mentioned this earlier, so if you reread my previous lines you might fall into the trap of thinking I'm "active." I didn't write anything in December. My illness explains certain things, particularly the physical pains that never leave me in peace, poignant, pointed, insurmountable. There is also a love affair, and many disenchantments that are finishing me off. But let's not talk about all that, I would like to talk to you only about beautiful things.

I want to ask a favour of you : please do not show the old

[6] Léon Pierre-Quint (1895-1958), born Léopold Léon Steindecker, writer, editor, literary critic, director of the Éditions du Sagittaire publishing house and early supporter of the Surrealist movement.

manuscripts I sent you to Léon Pierre-Quint, don't show them to anyone.

In a weekly newspaper, the kind one finds in a W.C., a guy whose stupidity I imagine is the crowning achievement of the genre publishes under a suggestive title some strangely beautiful poems that he vainly tries to pollute. One of them is yours, which I think is splendid : "Cinq pièces à vertige — immortellement désunies." I was a little saddened to have to read your work through an intermediary and would have loved to receive from you the magazines that have published your poems, and of course I would have sent them back to you without delay. But perhaps you consider our friendship too minor* — forgive this reproach, it was hard for me to write it. Perhaps you don't think it important whether or not I read what you write, and this would fill me with sadness. If I knew what magazines published your work I could easily get hold of them — but you never tell me — not even that.

I hope I can write you at greater length some other time; meanwhile, I send you all my friendship,

M. Blecher

*Please don't feel you have to defend yourself, I don't want to impose on you in the least.

P.S. I've just sent a letter to Léon Pierre-Quint, but after rereading yours I now realise I've made a faux-pas as he was only asking you to enquire about my projects rather than suggesting that I write to him directly. And this is exactly what I have done. Please explain to him that it was a misunderstanding.

P.P.S. I've just reread this letter. It's very different from the one I intended to write. But at the end of the day, it's just a letter where I send you "the latest news" about me.

LEYSIN, 8 MAY 1933

Dear Minet,

Tomorrow I leave for Romania. I'm composing a long letter for you in my mind, but if you feel like writing me first, here is my new address : 151 Strada Mare, Roman, Romania. Almost everything is going badly for me.

With all my friendship, affectionately yours,

M. Blecher

VIENNA, 12 MAY 1933

Dear Minet,

I am writing to you from Vienna to fill in the details that I alluded to in my postcard. I need a small favour — actually, a big one. If you write to L.P. Quint, please send him my new address: 151 Str. Mare, Roman, Romania. I'll write more soon. I lie here in my hotel room all day long. It's raining and I'm ravaged by fever.

M.B.

ROMAN, [22 MAY] 1933

Dear Minet,

I received your letter. Thank you. First of all, here are the answers to your questions. I haven't gone to the Black Sea coast yet. Roman is in the north of the Moldova region. I've gone back home to my family until I am admitted to the seaside sanatorium. It's quite difficult to get a place there even if you're able to afford it, but I have hope, because I know that some people are appealing on my behalf. So it looks like I'll be staying in Roman for two or three weeks, in *my* room, where I used to spend entire hours dreaming and hoping. I feel tortured by all the adolescence that still permeates the walls. It was a bad time and everything has only gotten worse since. There is something fundamentally evil in the world, a kind of vertigo that I feel growing and becoming more intense each day, every sore in my body ringing out clearly and fully at my touch, like the unmistakable tones of a piano. There is a presence here, no doubt about it. The walls of my room bear their decorations (I say "bear" because the walls are truly pregnant with flowers, with all the mystery that impregnates them), some large blue chrysanthemums floating on golden rivers, drawing me into a *neurasthenic hilarity,* which is just as tragic as any other. These chrysanthemums really do have an air of Greek tragedy and the modern clown. A reevaluation of all spiritual values. No crying allowed, because tears are just meaningless decoration; sometimes laughter says more. All this has surprised you. Sometimes I'm delirious with fever. I get agitated : my pillow feels hot : from me. You find this distasteful — these anatomical details, especially the body's external processes. I, too, find them distasteful, especially since you wrote me about it, because your friendship alters the way I perceive many things. That's the only change, and then there is reality, from which I no longer pull anything but my own *thread*. This is why the "feverish hallucinations" I described to you shouldn't be subjected to analytical madness. On the contrary. As I expand into these multiform dimensions, sometimes amorphous, sometimes with contours too firm for my liking (because "I am, I always am"), I "compose" a symphony. I haven't written a single line of it yet, it will come; you once told me that "the day will carry its own birth."

At the moment I have completed a manuscript that only needs to be edited. In two or three months I will send it, with no expectations, to L.P. Quint. The manuscript no longer reflects who I am, but maybe I don't even know anymore. Regardless, I don't believe it would be any better if I didn't consider it sincere. Let's leave it at that.

Dear Minet, please don't trouble yourself with my poems etc. I don't have anything that's ready, clean. Whatever I manage to finish I'll send to someone, somewhere, *so that it can exist*. I don't care about anything else. Whatever I send you is just an extension of my letters. I don't want anything from you. The friendship you show me would embarrass me if I thought it was a response to an appeal I unwittingly slipped into my letters. I realize this might verge on the inhuman and maybe a matter of overweening pride. Please don't think of it that way, Minet. When I write I reveal everything about myself. What might come across as pride is only my desire not to *force anyone's hand*.

Love : I am mired in night. Love must *serve me*. I'm expressing myself badly : serving in the sense of being mine. I understand you cannot mess around with sexuality. Though incomprehensible, sometimes we do mess around with it and flowers sprout — in the brain, everywhere. But love, true love, is something that becomes *me-myself* and indistinguishable from *me-myself.* I have left this behind in Leysin as if abandoning the mirror image of my heart. (You know what the heart means for me now : arteries and noise amplified in the ear : I "anatomise.")

A confession. I've got it. It has become a tradition that every letter I write to you must end with a confession that will *cost me dearly,* either for my pride, or for the aesthetics of sincerity etc. . . .

Today's : *in my letters I always try to paint myself in a favourable light.* Ah, how this confession pains me, Minet! Accept this gift from me. Do with it what you will.

With all my friendship,

M. Blecher

P.S. Money. I have enough money in Romania because all my uncles and aunts can give me money, whereas they could not send it to me while I was abroad. I will pay all the sanatorium fees with these gifts, so as to ease the burden on my parents.

ROMAN, 23 MAY 1933

Dear Minet,

I forgot to mention in the letter I wrote to you yesterday about a particular phrase of yours : "reality is nothing more than a trodden steppe . . ." — From the moment I read this, I felt it was true. Reflecting on it afterwards, I began to like it more and more, in the way I like all things I could have never come up with myself. The idea of a personal spectacle in a world that is completely indifferent and even depleted disturbs me a great deal. And then, I think only our passions could give us the *chance* at the harmony you dream of, and this thought obsesses me more and more each day, as a fulfilment, and as a perfection of the friendly gratitude I extend to you for this revelation.

M. Blecher

C.T.C. SANATORIUM, CARMEN SYLVA, CONSTANŢA COUNTY, ROMANIA, [SUMMER 1933]

Dear Minet,

I'm writing to you in a rush, before I've even received your reply, to let you know that my friend René Wauquier,[7] whom you know, will visit you in the next few days. He is a unique character, whose many qualities I didn't fully understand while I was in

[7] Belgian friend of Blecher who visited him several times and helped him out with publicity. "Grotesque Poem" is dedicated to him.

Berck. Of course, he still needs to temper his juvenile verbosity, but I believe by encouraging his sincerity and purity of expression he can create work of a high quality.

I've taken the liberty of asking him to deliver a parcel to you. Forgive my presumption.

I am now on the Black Sea coast, in a "climate" that is extraordinarily conducive to what I hope to achieve. At the same time, my treatment has begun in earnest and in the best hygienic conditions.

The sea is at my feet, the cliff looming directly over the waves. During the day I lie on the terrace with the other patients, although it is not crowded, and in the evening I sleep in my room.

I will write to you again, when I have something worth writing about. I remain your loyal friend,

M. Blecher

C.T.C. SANATORIUM, CARMEN SYLVA, CONSTANŢA COUNTY, ROMANIA, [SUMMER 1933]

My dear dear Minet,

How can I embrace you in a letter? How can I fail to love you a little more each day? Your rum-tinged letter is sublime. I can't resist hijinks, because deep down I'm a clown, and I'd like to rename my entire life "Enter the Comic" (what a fantastic title for a novel!) and would like to see all the men around me send their "personalities" to hell and honestly admit they're also clowns and promise to stop taking themselves so seriously and dance naked in the streets all in a fluster like "lovestruck fools." Long live the circus of our daily lives! And long live our moment of rest — poor thing — that weighs so heavily on the clown because nothing seems as if it would ever begin again. You know how ridiculous melancholy can sometimes be — *but here, it's pure sadness* . . . Down with the tired gaiety of polite anecdotes with "punchlines" — Let's take the risk of transforming our deepest tragedies into buffoonery . . . Ah, let's all be a little more honest! I love you, Minet, but please don't give up — don't quit the racetrack. I have a small circle of spectators here; I think they see me as a little crazy, yet amusing; in the evenings I feel like applauding myself. But for God's sake, I can't help it — I've brought a few stuffy fellows down a peg or two, the assassination game is a stupid one, though I have it "in my blood."

Please forgive me if this doesn't make any sense to you. Look, I'm kneeling before you, lit candle in hand, waiting for a word from you.

I am also enclosing some photographs with captions, so they do not arrive to you deaf and dumb. Please confirm your receipt of these either by writing to me directly or through Wauquier. Thanks.

Wauquier will bring you several pages I've written — I'm not sure when. They are some poems and also some reflections on the reality I'm living — simple stories that have poured through my fingers — without any other significance except for their variety. If they give you a moment's entertainment, that's good enough for me.

But I fear you will also find in them things you won't like. Once again, I beg your forgiveness. To paraphrase myself (you'll see), I invest myself in what I can create in my own extraordinary way "as such." Such and such, for God's sake, I'm confused, damn these pages, do with them what you will — I think *La Ville* might publish them. But I'm already regretting this poor presentation.

Anxiously awaiting your verdict, forever yours,

M. Blecher

[TECHIRGHIOL], 16 MARCH 1934

Dear Mr. Saşa Pană,[8]

Please forgive my presumption for writing to you without us having been introduced. But how else can I send you a message expressing my profound admiration? I have just finished reading *Diagrams* and *The Romanticised Life of God,* iridescent hourglasses, lights in my shadow. It would be a miracle if I could make your acquaintance : would you accept an invitation to come to visit me for a few days?

By way of introduction : in no. 6 of Breton's *Le surréalisme ASDLR*, on page 25, you will find a poem of mine;[9] I am also sending you the beginning of a long poem entitled "Nightfall" and two drawings, one of which is a self-portrait.[10]

I look forward to your reply.

With greatest respect,

M. Blecher

---

[8] The pen name of Alexandru Binder (1902-81), born into a Bucharest Jewish family and educated as a physician in Iaşi, he was one of the major figures of the Romanian interwar avant-garde. Influenced by Dada and Surrealism, Pană founded and edited the magazine *unu* in 1928, which was also a publishing house (Editura Unu) that put out works by such seminal Romanian modernists as Urmuz, Tristan Tazara, Stephan Roll, Ilarie Voronca and others, and he was instrumental in getting Blecher's only collection of poetry, *Transparent Body*, published. The two early Surrealist inspired collections of his prose poetry mentioned here were both published by Editura Unu (as *Diagrame* (1930) and *Viața romanțata a lui dumnezeu* (1932)) and are included in a collection of Pană's interwar writing forthcoming in English translation from Twisted Spoon Press.

[9] "The Inextricable Position" first appeared in French in *Le Surréalisme au service de la révolution,* no. 6 (1933).

[10] The poem "Se face noapte" was to be published by Editura Unu with drawings from Sandu Haymovici, but the project never materialized. Pană notes that he sent the poem and self-portrait to André Breton.

[TECHIRGHIOL, 1934]

Mihail Bera,[11]

He is twenty-four years old.

He is alive.

He lives by the sea, in the sun, he wanders through yards tinged with nostalgia and pavements licked clean of dust. He spots a girl, a dog or a shell : he gazes at them; he doesn't know anything; he doesn't understand anything; the contours of a dream slip straight through his fingers into the full absurdity of reality.

His whirlwinds cannot be compressed in a drawer and his ships scatter apart as they sail.

In the vacuum of four white walls, he sculpts his multifarious body. With hallucinatory precision, he exists. His life is fixedly determined because it can only continue like *this*.

He writes his drafts underneath the skin before transferring them onto paper.

C.T.C. Sanatorium
Carmen Sylva
Constanța County

[TECHIRGHIOL], 9 APRIL 1934

Dearest Mr. Sașa Pană,

The last few days have been very difficult and full of commotion, so please forgive my tardy reply. My friendship flows towards you unabated after reading your sensitive and sympathetic

[11] Blecher uses a pseudonym of his own invention here for Geo Bogza (1908-93), one of the most important interwar Romanian avant-garde poets and early Surrealists. He and his wife Elisabeta (Elly) met Blecher for the first time when they visited him in Brașov in 1934. The bulk of Blecher's extant correspondence over 1934-38 is addressed to them.

analysis of my work. Since then, my fantasies of us meeting in person have brightened the hours of my daily existence. They sprung up in my mind the moment I heard from you, like roses or rays of light. Your letter is the best I could have hoped for.

I'd be grateful if you could also thank Geo Bogza for the postcard he sent me. Some bizarre mania for disguise and subterfuge compelled me to substitute a pseudonym for his name. Please reestablish the truth.

I'm obsessed by the thought of your paying me a visit. I will be leaving this place in May — I'm not yet sure where I'll be going next. I would be delighted if you could visit me here before then. Everything would be easier and simpler : it's enough to tell me the date of your arrival and I'll make sure a room is ready for you.

Mrs. Bălăcescu[12] has asked me to thank you for the lines addressed to her in your letter. I've come up with an idea for a kind of "trade," if you wish to accept it. Here it is : given you're such an admirer of her drawings and she likes your poems, it should be a simple matter to agree to an exchange of one of her paintings for one of your books. However, at the moment I can't go to see her to suggest this deal because she's very ill — the doctors think it might be erysipelas — and she is not allowed any visitors.

I can't wait to meet you in person and I'm sending my regards, along with all my friendship and admiration,

M. Blecher

[12] Lucia Demetriade-Bălăcescu (1895-1979), a painter who was receiving treatment at the sanatorium in Techirghiol at the same time as Blecher. The two collaborated on an exhibition catalogue.

[BUCHAREST], 3 MAY 1934

Dearest Mr. Pană,

On the way to Brașov. I will be here for twelve hours and am staying at Hotel Imperial. It would give me immeasurable pleasure if you could visit me at 5 in the afternoon.

Please be so kind as to let me know if you are able to come.

Sending you all the morning's freshness,

M. Blecher

BRAŞOV, [5 JUNE 1934]

My dear Mr. Bogza,

Thank you so much for taking an interest in my poems. When you last spoke to Hay,[13] I think he hadn't received a definite answer from me yet, but now everything has been arranged and *Transparent Body* will be out soon.

So yes, of course you may announce this in *Vremea* [The Times],[14] I'm sure a couple of lines will do.

Over the last few days I've managed to get some writing done.

Yesterday I saw an announcement in *Vremea* for your forthcoming article "Report from an Airplane."

We are preparing your room here and I think you'll be comfortable. Mrs. Martin has gone to a great deal of trouble.

---

[13] Sandu Haymovici [Haimovici] (1908-91), also known as Sandu Hay, visual artist, painter, sculptor, Blecher's friend from childhood. Emigrated to Cuba in 1941 and made a name as the visual artist Sandú Darié.

[14] Bucharest-based national newspaper published between 1928 and 1938. The listed publication date for *Transparent Body* is May 1934 (Editura Bibliofila), yet the announcement that ran in *Vremea* on 10 June 1934 stated it was "to appear in a few days."

Please write to me before you arrive so I can make sure everything is in order.

Your devoted friend,

M. Blecher

8 STR. CIOCRAC, BRAŞOV, ROMANIA, [JUNE/JULY] 1934

Dear Minet,

Here, at last, is *Transparent Body,* the booklet Wauquier must have told you about. I haven't written to you for a while because I was ashamed to present myself to you empty-handed, you know how much I detest idleness, and especially the idea of living my whole life as a dilettante. I'm currently working on something more "serious." The opening section is finished. Nevertheless, it's rather hard going, I have to pull tight on the reins to keep my ideas on the right track. I keep repeating to myself your words about harmony. You are right, we should keep our follies close together (my loose interpretation).

I have taken the liberty of dedicating a poem to you and I'm sending you its translation. I dedicated my heart to you long ago.

I'm not in great shape at the moment, I have a constant fever and these wretched fistulas won't stop suppurating. So here are the few words for today — I will await a letter from you to learn if you're annoyed by my silence. Write to me how you're doing, what you're working on, and anything else that might interest me.

I forgot to mention that I'm writing reviews for serious journals and that my poems have been published in less serious magazines. Of course, I have no illusions on that front, I would need a few years of scribbling before I could claim to have "found" my voice; it's hard when fever makes you feel as if your head is about to explode and poisons all your sentences with its little nauseating odours (ah, fever is an opaque, viscous liquid, its ooze like the movements of an octopus).

Write to me, dear Minet, you are at the seaside, you can see the little boats with their petal-like sails and the protean sea, dark brown, then clear, then cloudy as lye (you could almost kiss it).

Forever yours,

like one of the little boats,

M. Blecher

[BRAŞOV], FRIDAY, 7 JULY 1934

Dearest Mr. Saşa Pană,

Your letter has brought me immeasurable joy. I recognised the envelope from afar, *unu* reminding me of a bird struggling to escape the fist of the postman so that it can fly towards me. Long silences weigh heavily upon me — they torment me and fill my head with phantoms. When you get to know me better, you will see this is in fact a budding persecution complex, a serious condition based on false assumptions. My illness is making me an expert in emotion and susceptibility — I've reached the stage I've feared most : *assister à sa propre degringolade.*

In any case, the letter I received from you this morning has, like a shaft of light, dispelled one particular obsession, for which I thank you. Here is what I have to say about my affinity to *unu*.

For me, the irreality and illogicality of daily life are no longer vague concepts reserved for intellectual speculation; I *live* this irreality and its fantastical elements. The first freedom I allowed myself was that of the irresponsibility of my inner actions towards each other — I've tried to tear down the barrier of consequences and — as a way of being honest with myself — have sought to valorize every temptation to the hallucinatory to the level of the lucid and voluntary. But *I don't know,* nor could I know, if the tentacles of Surrealism are developing inside me, or how fast. All I know is that I will play the game until I run out of pieces. I would like to think that from now till eternity a handful of poets, like true vampires preying on bloated consciences and putrid ideas, will suck out the blood of quietude and fly like banners the shadows of the most precious, most digestible, most moral illusions of humanity.

My ideal of writing would be to transpose into literature the high tension found in a Salvador Dalí painting. That cool dementia, perfectly legible and essential, is what I would like to achieve. Explosions between the walls of my room and not at a distance between chimerical and abstract continents.

The visit of spectres should occur in a normal manner, with a polite knock on the door followed by a polite strangulation. Surrealism should hurt like a deep wound.

On some points, however, I feel I diverge from the pure orthodoxy of the Manifesto, so the question remains if *unu* could accommodate my perspective or would expect me to change it.

I am trying to express this in *Exercises in Immediate Irreality.*[15] I will send you a few pages and if you read them in a generous state of mind you might find the novel has some merits. I feel like I'm working in a bottomless mine with my head poisoned by fever, tormented by the fact that my manuscript is not coming together in the way I'd like it to.

From time to time I write a poem for my chapbook collection *The Grass of Dreams,* which I am hoping will come out this autumn.

---

[15] The manuscript title of Blecher's first novel that was eventually published as *Adventures in Immediate Irreality* in 1936.

I want to ask you a favour : when I was staying in Carmen Sylva I sent you a few pages of a poem called "Nightfall." Since it was my only copy, I would be grateful if you could return these pages to me so I can add them to the rest of the poem, which I would like to type up in the next few days. I will make a copy for you. Hay has created a few illustrations that should be printed with the poem.

So that's everything I will be working on this summer : *Exercises*; *The Grass of Dreams*; and "Nightfall"; but everything is going slowly, unbelievably slowly, fever deadens me and I lie for hours like an animal stunned by a blow to the head.

That's all for today, except to say : your letter has calmed me and plucked a weed out of my soul.

I send you my friendship and boundless admiration.

M. Blecher

P.S. I'm also including two drawings that you are welcome to keep.

[BRAŞOV], 15 JULY 1934

Dear Mr. Sașa Pană,

I am writing this quickly so that my letter reaches you by tomorrow (Sunday) in Bucharest.

I can confirm that I've received the manuscript and thank you very much for sending it.

I keep working on *Exercises* with a kind of feverish intensity. The first chapters are likely to be ready in a few weeks, I think. The book is growing, its proportions swelling like a protean being : *never before have I written anything with so much "passion."*

Transparent Body was only the beginning, and I no longer recognise myself in it. The only reason I still love it is because it contains part of my heart.

My friendship floats towards you like a white scarf,
M. Blecher

[BRAŞOV], 21 AUGUST 1934

Dearest Sașa Pană,

This month has been a difficult one for me, first due to my illness, then my low morale, so I feel rather broken. But I keep working on my book : it's like an island to which I run, heart heavy like a rain cloud, and return purified, almost softened.

I would like to ask you for a favour that would give me a great deal of joy, if it's not too much trouble : I would like to have a look at the entire collection of *unu*, as I've only read a few issues. When you return to Bucharest, could you lend it to me for one or two weeks? Obviously, I'll take great care of it and return it to you as soon as I can. But I repeat, only if it's not too much trouble.

And now I'm appealing to your expertise as a doctor and would be grateful if you could tell me everything you know about choline hydroxide as a treatment to improve general health. What is your opinion of it and are there any contraindications?

Many thanks, I send you all my friendship and a fistful of this morning's ineffable blue sky.

M.B.

[BRAŞOV], 8 OCTOBER 1934

Dearest Sașa Pană,

I am leaving Brașov in two days and my new address will be 151 Ștefan cel Mare Street, Roman. It would give me immeasurable pleasure if you could send me the *unu* collection you promised, which I will naturally treat with utmost care and send back to you as soon as possible.

With my warmest regards,

M. Blecher

[ROMAN, OCTOBER 1934]

Dear Geo Bogza, the great Geo Bogza, my beloved Geo Bogza,

Here I am in my room, ready to write to you first and foremost a few lines to express all my satisfaction and warm gratitude for your loving care of me in Brașov.

Life is only worth living for these rare and sublime encounters. And here I am speaking of the sublime after a journey that not only shook me physically but also greatly affected my morale and, for a while, stripped all my actions, judgments, and aspirations of meaning.

My beloved Geo Bogza,

Forgive me, I beg you, forgive me for telling you so openly that our relationship is among those truly rare "events" in my life that are and will remain sublime. Forgive me for using this word, which I expect will embarrass you. When I met Marie,[16] I wrote to her confessing all my love, a love that has lasted to this day. I'm telling you this so you don't think these lines are born out of a passing enthusiasm; my affection is always carefully considered and unshakable. You know I could write reams about the love and gratitude I feel for you. However, I will stop before I embarrass you further. You can fill in the gaps yourself, *as tastefully as possible.*

About my journey : the train compartment was empty the

[16] Maria Ghiolu, wife of the industrialist Stavri Ghiolu, is also mentioned in Mihail Sebastian's *Journal.*

whole way because I rode first class from Ploiești, but at the stations, it was the most infernal torment to get on and off, although I had a stretcher at both Ploiești and Roman. All my bones are crushed, and the fact that I found a wonderful room here with a terrace, sun, light, space, and cleanliness (all of them superlative) is the only thing that slightly lifts me from the "pit" into which I've sunk.

I will write more to you tomorrow. Right now, I'm tired and going to bed.

Everything I wrote at the beginning of this letter about my feelings for you applies to Elly as well, absolutely everything. I kiss you both.

M. Blecher

P.S. I love you, but I'm too tired, I'll write more tomorrow.

[ROMAN], 12 OCTOBER 1934

My beloved Geo and Elly,

I'm writing you just a postcard because today I've been overwhelmed by exhaustion. It's probably the effect of returning to normal life; I'm feeling a little less tired now, because I've spent this morning on the terrace and the fresh air has invigorated me. My sister's house is far from the centre of town — no noise or dust here. My brother-in-law and sister are extraordinarily kind and helpful. They've even provided me with a room where I can receive guests. Both my house and my heart are ready to welcome you. Come to me whenever you want and stay as long as you like. The excruciating pain in my chest muscles has eased a bit.

Sending you kisses, I will write more later,

M. Blecher

P.S. Needless to say, I am still troubled by what's transpiring in

Brașov, please write to me to let me know how everything has turned out.

[ROMAN], 14 OCTOBER 1934

My beloved Geo and Elly,

I have received all the postcards and I'm grateful to you because I think of them as protoplasmic threads that keep us connected. Here are some things I want to write to you about, in no particular order. Where am I staying? I'm at my sister's place at the moment, where I have a splendid room with light coloured walls, parquet flooring, a good stove, a large window, a separate entrance, a direct door to an enormous terrace, a porcelain washbasin with running water, in short, a room that rivals any chamber in the largest Swiss sanatorium in terms of hygiene and aesthetics, so that the only thing I'm missing is the altitude, but the air here is very clean because the terrace overlooks a garden with walnut trees and on the side of the house you can stare out into the open horizon.

I will photograph everything and send you the pictures. I'm a bit ashamed (and when I have a fever, I feel overcome by a nausea for myself and for everything that exists), that I've been blessed with this comfortable situation when others are struggling, but won't continue with these kind of musings lest they should become too literary.

Here is a rough floor plan of the house :

Entrance hall
Door
Stove
Bookcase
MY ROOM

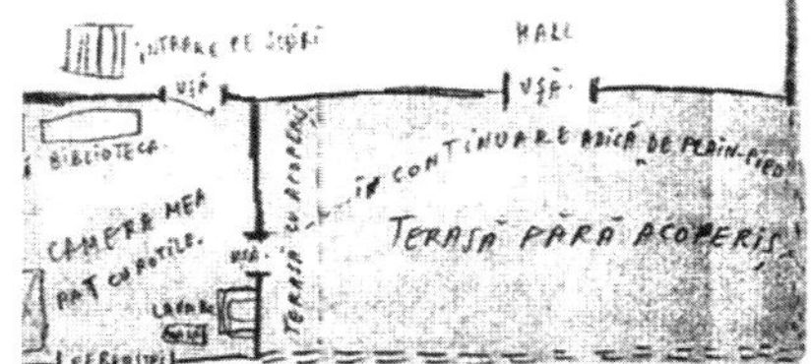

Wheeled bed
Table
Hall
Covered terrace
Door
Door
. . . leading to . . .
UNCOVERED TERRACE
Window
Bathroom

There are no stairs anywhere : I can get to the terrace from my room easily, no steps at all. As far as food goes, they will bring me anything I fancy. My sister and brother-in-law have welcomed me with boundless love and kindness. They will do anything for me and go out of their way to ensure that I don't exhaust myself, that nothing irritates me, so that I can live peacefully.

For example, my brother-in-law has brought me some clay from his factory so that I can make figurines. I'll send a few to you after they've been fired in the kiln, if they come out all right.

He also brings me all the books I want, he's basically like a brother to me, so considerate and attentive to all my needs.

He encouraged me (not out of mere politeness, but wholeheartedly) to invite anyone I want to the house. We have a spare room, so if you or Elly or both of you want to come, you have a place to stay for as long as you *want*.

Please buy me *a hundred* envelopes, if it's not too much trouble — exactly like the one that encloses this letter — from the Cartea Românească bookshop in Brașov and send them to me. I will pay you back later, just keep track of everything you spend on me.

I've been struggling to write of late. I'm still very tired and in the evenings a fever sets my whole body on fire.

Please apologise to Cantonieru[17] that I haven't written to him yet, I barely write anything as I get all hot and my hand starts to hurt. When I first arrived here, my whole body used to ache, but now most of the pain has settled in a leg.

My own house will be ready in a month or maybe even later. I am sending you a postcard that followed me from Brașov, look at how the postman scribbled on it "forward," it should have been an exclamation : "forwarrrd!!!"

I look forward to seeing you, come visit soon, sending you greetings and kisses,

M. Blecher

P.S. Forgive this abominable letter. I will send it to your address in Bucharest.

[ROMAN], 17 OCTOBER 1934

Dear Geo Bogza,

I am enclosing the poem with all the final modifications. I was very tired when I copied it, and perhaps its calligraphic appearance leaves something to be desired, but I can't bring myself to rewrite it. I've also come to think that it will be difficult to place it in *Vremea*. I realised this as I was writing it out. The last issue

[17] Niculae Cantonieru (1899-1935), short-story writer, novelist, and editor of *Frize*.

of *Vremea* ran a poem that is miles away from "Paris" in terms of style and form, presumably the type Pompiliu Constantinescu[18] likes, and in that case he will decline to publish my poem.

Anyway, if it comes to that, please don't worry. I told you my feelings about getting my work published : if it happens, great, but if it doesn't, that's fine too.

I was terribly sorry I couldn't see Voronca.[19] Thank you once again for all the many ways you show me sympathy. Each proof of it falls on a ground that burns like a glowing coal and touches my deepest, most intimate feelings.

I'm not reading very much — *Le Grand Meaulnes*[20] (rereading) and the newspapers. It is impossible for me to write a single line until I feel better. An undefined weariness pervades me, a kind of numbing stupor that saps my strength. But I believe a regimen of abundant food and fresh air will have me feeling better in a few weeks. Unusually for me, yesterday I sat on the terrace facing the street : Roman is a rotten town full of rotten people, inside and out, especially *inside*. I keep myself isolated in my room, I don't receive any visitors — neither relatives nor acquaintances.

I get along best with my sister and brother-in-law.

The weather is autumnal, with a dreadfully oppressive ceiling of clouds and a vague, interminable grey light.

Every day, I realise more and more how essential our meeting has been to my life. You are the expression of the strong, *fundamental*, granite world, and you have brought into my sphere of

---

[18] (1901-46), literary critic and editor.

[19] Ilarie Voronca, born Eduard Marcus (1903-46) into a Jewish family, was an important Romanian avant-garde writer of poetry and stories who switched to writing in French after moving to Paris in 1933.

[20] Published in 1913, the only novel by Alain-Fournier.

knowledge the reality it lacked. Not only intellectually, but also in terms of my illness and my life in general.

With lots of love,

M. Blecher

Please give my warmest regards to Elly, the pure one.

P.S. I wrote to you in Brașov asking you to buy me a hundred envelopes identical to this one, but maybe you didn't have time. Please buy them for me in Bucharest, also from Cartea Românească, and I will reimburse you the cost. Thank you.

ROMAN, 27 OCTOBER 1934

Dear Geo Bogza,

You can imagine, of course, how moved I was when I opened *Frize* and read your poem;[21] but I doubt you can imagine the exact quality of this emotion and especially its hidden depths, a feeling that cannot be put into words and takes on a life of its own, beginning as a warm sensation rolling along the heart and then suddenly transforming into purified breath, as if the whole body finds a long sought purpose. This morning, my body and organs discovered the meaning of this poem : it was friendship. I treasure it inside me, unbroken.

But these are just words, we ought instead to communicate what we have to say with splendid pieces of roasted meat or with cheap ribbons like the ones maidservants buy, or with the soundtrack of a documentary about the Forestry Commission, capturing the raising of the axe, the sudden shudder of wood, and lumberjacks in slightly tattered khaki trousers, the cord of their underpants dangling on their bare legs. I watched such an event

[21] Bogza's poem "De vorbă cu M. Blecher" [Speaking with M. Blecher] appeared in *Frize* on 1 November 1934.

all afternoon from my terrace today. And you know perfectly well that I'm not describing it to you because it represents something extraordinary, but precisely because it's not extraordinary at all.

I'm finding it hard to write, it is evening, sleep is gluing my eyelids together. As I've already mentioned, I spent all day on the terrace, and I've developed a slight fever from the sun.

Everything continues for me as usual, but I'm burdened with fatigue. In comparison to Brașov, life here is whiter, clearer, but I feel more tired. Sometimes I'm overcome by a deep sense of revulsion. It comes directly from this clarity, which is generally bearable because it is born out of silence and isolation and not part of any kind of mystical-philosophical-literary scaffolding.

My brother-in-law and sister continue to treat me in the same benignly oblivious manner that is the only form of behaviour I can tolerate. When I move to my own house I will be even less involved in family life — a kind of life I detest, even though I possess only the warmest feelings of love for my dear parents who do everything for me as if seized by a *religious fervour*.

I realise this letter falls desperately short of the depth of feeling you expressed in your poem. But, as well as your other many qualities, I hope you don't mind my saying that I find you very easy to confide in. You are like a *comfortable* armchair, "the person" to whom I can write anything and who will fill in the gaps and order these ideas for himself. Please do the same with this letter.

Kisses to you and Elly.

Yours,

M. Blecher

[ROMAN,] 4 NOVEMBER 1934

Dear Minet,

Here is my new address : 151 Strada Mare, Roman, Romania.

It is my parents' address, but I don't live with them, instead I occupy a perfectly isolated room with a terrace in my sister's home while I wait to relocate to *my* own house on the "outskirts" of town, a small, clean, new house full of light, surrounded by a garden full of trees and flowers.

This is all I can write to you about the "essentials" of my life, with its immutable exactitude : eating, sleeping, sun, bedroom.

As for the other, "mad" life, I feel myself faltering, but I'm still working and have almost finished my book. It will probably come out at the beginning of next year. It is taking shape all by itself and above all has astonishingly "simplified"; the important thing is that I keep writing and not preconceive it — "thinking" too much about a book is a sure way to destroy it from the outset, and that's why now I only dream and construct when I have a piece of paper in front of me. And then there is also the indescribable satisfaction of having achieved something; it is a cerebral spasm, a calm, clear convulsion.

You will find enclosed a poem by a renowned young poet named Geo Bogza, whose work is much admired. It has just been published in a literary magazine in Romania and was a wonderful surprise for me.

Let me know if you like it; don't be taken aback by the *Catholic* motifs. Bogza is the world's greatest non-conformist. He was recently put on trial for his *Invective Poem*, an incredibly vigorous, powerful book that the courts condemned as "pornographic." Needless to say, they didn't understand Bogza's poetry, its masculine power and ferocious sexuality, yet of extraordinary purity and infinite humanity.[22]

And how are you, dear Minet? Is it really impossible that you should walk into my room one morning with a magnificent smile and bare neck (looking so cool, so cool, ah, how *cool* you are, Minet) just in shirtsleeves? What a beautiful dream, the most beautiful of my entire "collection."

I have just written a long article about Berck, *for money*, for a Romanian newspaper.[23] Would you like me to translate it for you? I repeat : I wrote this article for a *fee*, therefore it is of scant literary merit. I continue to collaborate with various poetry magazines.

Yours, with my whole ♥

M. Blecher

[Blecher's French translation of Geo Bogza's poem "Speaking with Max Blecher" follows.]

[ROMAN], 4 NOVEMBER 1934

Dear Mr. Sașa Pană,

Reading *The Funicular Ride*[24] as autumn turns everything around me crimson and gold was like embarking on a fantastical journey through the filigreed cascades of imagery of a superior poem.

---

[22] Geo Bogza was twice brought up on pornography charges ("priapism") : the first in 1932 for his collection *Sex Diary* (1929), for which he was acquitted at trial; the second for *Invective Poem* (1933), for which he was sentenced to six days in jail in February 1934, though litigation dragged on for years, prompting Blecher to ask him how the trial was going in a letter on 3 November 1934. (Bogza was incarcerated again in 1937 for the same text and on the same pretext, at a time when similar charges also landed fellow Surrealist Gherasim Luca in jail.)

[23] "Berck, Kingdom of the Damned," appeared in *Vremea* on 7 October 1934.

[24] Pană's poetry collection *Călătorie cu funicularul* (Bucharest: Editura Unu, 1934).

I would like to congratulate you, but first of all I'd like to thank you for giving me the pleasure of taking me on this journey through the landscape of the poem.

Many thanks also for the *unu* collection, which I will return to you without delay in the next few days. I've leafed through it carefully (without cutting the pages, of course) and felt connected with the living spirit of Romanian modernism in a way that I have missed by being abroad for a few years. I look forward to further issues of the magazine.

Cordially,

M. Blecher

ROMAN, 9 NOVEMBER 1934

My dear Geo and Elly,

All morning I've been tinkering with an old radio set, screwing and unscrewing it to get it to work properly. Yesterday I flicked through several collections of magazines and newspapers from a few years ago, yellow with age. I don't remember what I did on Tuesday. Every day I find some task that I convince myself needs to be done, and that's how time passes for me, in a sort of active laziness that keeps me away from writing and correspondence. Yet I feel a strong reaction growing inside me and when it finally explodes, I will return to *Exercises* for a few days, and maybe I will complete it. I'm starting to shape the text as it should be presented to a real reader, making no concessions, I just want the book to feel as clear and cohesive as possible. We'll see how it turns out.

Just this morning I received your postcard, which moved me. When are you coming to Roman? My house will be ready in a few days, and perhaps I will then move into it. Only one room is fully finished, the one I'll be in. I left the others as is and will get to them in spring.

My sister tells me one of the rooms is painted entirely in dark red; of course, I'll leave it like that. The previous owner was an armourer whose conversational range was limited to the question of "is it or is it not?" — a tall, pale man with a small bureaucratic moustache, and I would have never suspected him of choosing that fantastical red colour for the room, but perhaps he chose it at random without any thought for aesthetics.

My health is not particularly great at the moment; cleanliness and good food are my lifelines, especially cleanliness. When I sweat, I change the sheets, the pillows are regularly aired out, the room is thoroughly cleaned — all of this gives me great pleasure, as I feel nostalgic for Switzerland and its clean white beds, immaculate rooms. Perhaps if I were healthy none of that would matter to me because ultimately such things are of little importance.

Please let me know your next court date.

I'm enclosing two photographs, one of them with my sister on her terrace.

I will stop here. I feel a slight fever coming on, probably because I've spent too much time writing. It's 5 o'clock in the afternoon, the window is open, and through the branches of the walnut tree I can see the field, grey and green, faded. It's an atmosphere of provincial uselessness and undefined melancholy.

Here's a stupid, sentimental letter.

Sending you many loving kisses,

M. Blecher

P.S. Important : When can I start writing to the new address? Please let me know.

ROMAN, 25 DECEMBER 1934

My beloved Geo and Elly,

I sent you a letter and a postcard to Burghelea Street, and just now another postcard to *Vremea*. I'm always waiting for you, and I hope your silence for so many days means you're preparing a surprise for me.

Vremea arrived in Roman yesterday, and I was thrilled to see the poem in print.[25] It's far beyond my expectations, and I thank Geo a thousand times for it. I feel jubilant to see it there, my only joy at the moment, apart from, of course, the thought that you will soon come to visit me in my home.

How wonderful it would be to hear a knock on the door, and when I ask who it is, to hear you say slowly and measuredly, "It's me, Geo Bogza, with Elly."

How good it would be, how splendid it would be.

Sending you kisses with longing,

M. Blecher

ROMAN, 26 DECEMBER 1934

Dear Geo,

I'm very sorry you won't be able to come, but I completely understand and hope we will see each other someday. My Christmas was a nightmare. My sister, who came from Iași, had cholecystitis (a terrible flare up of the liver), and we were all in a panic. She's better now, but I was very worried. I love her immensely, and I suffered a lot when I saw her in such pain.

Nothing new otherwise. Sandu Haymovici is in Roman and stops by often . . .

---

[25] "Paris" first appeared in *Vremea* on 24 December 1934.

I'm glad things are looking more hopeful with regard to your trip abroad.

I can see from your letters that you're under a lot of stress. These are chaotic, terrifying days, and I know the most recent events in particular must have been terribly difficult for you to deal with.

I think I'll move in a few days and then I'll have complete solitude and should be able to focus on finishing *Exercises*.

With much love and kisses to you and Elly,

M. Blecher

P.S. Just now, Silviu Roda[26] came to tell me that he went to *Vremea* a few times to look for you *on my behalf*. . . ! I was completely stunned. I never sent him to you; this is all on his own volition.

[ROMAN], 24 FEBRUARY 1935

Dearest Dory and Saul,[27]

A few days ago, Uncle Saul came over from Bucharest and brought me some of your letters, which I read with great interest and which, I have to confess, touched me a great deal. It sounds like you've embarked on an admirable new life there, full of power and vitality. I know you've encountered some hardships, yet by conquering them you seem to have found a joy that makes up for the exhaustion. Young people here lead dull lives, insipid to the point of exasperation, without any passion or ideals. Their pastimes are nothing but the stupid and desperate search for a few hours of oblivion. Your life there, on the other hand, is more

[26] (1916-39), poet and prose writer from Roman, and regular magazine contributor.

[27] Saul Schwartz was Blecher's cousin who had emigrated to Palestine with his wife. The sign-off "Maniu" was a nickname used only among family members.

human, more elemental, profoundly connected to the earth; those are the greatest [illegible] that life has to offer.

I wish you all the best from my urban cell, stuffed with mouldy, useless civilisation.

Kisses to you both,

Maniu

ROMAN, 4 MARCH 1935

Dear Geo Bogza,

Thank you very much for taking care of my essay.[28] To be honest, I can see now that by getting rid of those quotes the text has become more dense and concise. In any case, you have given me great joy; it's my first published essay.

Now, regarding all my literary "projects" : I haven't finished *Exercises*. If I had really pushed myself, the book could have been published this spring, but I was afraid that by writing under pressure, without having the time to make numerous revisions, I would end up with something of inferior quality. As you always adamantly insist, I must create something *good*, from the heart. I still have about 100 pages to transcribe (100 are already done), then I will leave everything aside for about a month and write the third version, which might be the final one. That will be around June or July, so *Exercises* could be published in autumn.

Please let me know if this "plan" sounds good to you. I want to produce something truly worthy of the trust you have placed in me. Your opinion matters more to me than anything else in

[28] Blecher's article "Care este esenţei poeziei?" [What Is the Essence of Poetry] appeared in *Vremea* on 3 March 1935, in which he concluded that Geo Bogza's *Invective Poem* was a powerful example of the strain in modern poetry of seething revolt against injustice, inequality, and stupid conventionalism.

the world, and if it's true that "we always write for someone," then *Exercises* is written for you.

In the meantime, I intend to write a few more articles or reports so that by autumn the reader will have come across my name four or five times. The article about William Blake is ready, and I think it's interesting. His life was full of cruel blows and sublime ecstasies. And he was obsessed by the idea of death, funerary decorations in particular, and this made me feel close to him and reminded me of the themes of my book. So I'm pleased to have written the article, even if it's not worthy of publication (I wrote it in parallel with all my other projects).

The article is accompanied by a substantial set of interesting reproductions. I will send you everything and you can judge for yourself.

But I worry you might find it a nuisance always having to make the submissions to *Vremea* for me, so please let me know if this is the case and I'll stop imposing on you.

Now, about other matters : I'm writing to you from my new room. I told you about the move in a postcard, I think. It's very good here, except that last night a massive blizzard suddenly started, and as I had turned off my heating in the evening, I was frozen to the bone by morning; the cold made my stomach and back seriously ache. Eventually the room warmed up throughout the morning and I thawed out, so now I've started to feel human again.

The room next to mine is waiting for you and Elly : I would like you to stay here all summer. Just this morning, my mother told me that she "hopes Geo Bogza is going to be comfortable here."

I really think you will; there won't be any more blizzards, and I don't foresee any other inconveniences.

Everyone who visits admires the house, the garden, and especially the system that I established from the first days to keep everything clean. It's on the edge of town, but more spacious, brighter, and more pleasant than other houses in the centre.

Anyway, I don't want to bore you with overly insistent invitations; but please believe that it would give me immense, indescribable pleasure if you and Elly could stay here for a few months.

Everything is futile, everything is unimportant, the only thing that matters in life is seeing friends, a joy as fine as air, a joy I can literally "inhale."

Lots of love and kisses to you and Elly,

M. Blecher

[ROMAN], 15 MAY 1935

Dear Mr. Sașa Pană,

I've been quite ill over the past few days; a terrible bout of enterocolitis has tormented me with severe pain and left me feeling very weakened. Once I start eating properly again, I think I'll begin to feel better. This is the reason why it took me so long to reply to your kind and generous letter as well as the proposition you made in it. However, I have no energy for literary endeavours at the moment, as I'm sure you can imagine. When I feel better, I will write to you again to discuss it. I should also add that *Exercises* is not finished and that recently I've felt so vanquished by my illness that I've been unable to make any progress on it.[29]

[29] Pană apparently had proposed to Blecher that Editura Unu publish another volume of his poetry. But Blecher was reluctant to consent because of a falling out between Bogza and Pană when the latter (having adopted Breton's approach) "excommunicated" Ilarie Voronca and two others from the proto-Surrealist group around *unu*. Bogza was unequivocally opposed to such action, and any reservations Blecher had about collaborating with Pană were likely informed by his loyalty to Bogza (see letter from 26 June 1936 below). It is worth noting that the *unu* group gave rise to the *Alge* group, whose members in turn formed (in 1940) the Surrealist Group of Romania.

I'm absolutely delighted that you want to visit me and I would like you to come when I've gotten my strength back and can talk to you lucidly without any worries, which I wish could be my natural state of mind.

I will expect you next month then, by which time I hope to have recovered. Until then I send you my warmest regards.

M. Blecher

ROMAN, 13 AUGUST 1935

Dear Geo Bogza,

I started writing to you as soon as I received your postcard on Monday, even though I don't yet have your address. There's no need for you to apologise, I am also miserable and plagued by a whole host of troubles that exasperate me beyond words and prevent me from writing to you more often. First and foremost, this excessive heat destroys me, irritates me, and drives me crazy. Then there's my stomach, which doesn't give me a moment's peace, followed by sleepless nights, the desire to finish the book, so basically, my dear Geo, my situation is hellish and I will breathe a sigh of relief when autumn finally arrives.

Forgive all this whingeing. But what can I do? Whom else should I tell all this to? One night, in a fit of exasperation, I tore my clothes off. I thought I would explode, I had to take sedatives and immerse my hands in cold water to calm down a little. I'm going through a very bad time.

As for *Exercises*, the book is finished, I just need to type it up. I have very little left to transcribe, so that's no problem. What troubles me is that *I don't know what I've written*, I don't know whether it's good or bad, I'm tormented by the idea that even though it's finished, I haven't included everything I wanted. But it's impossible for me to write anymore.

You have offered to come over at some point to read it. My infinite thanks. Maybe by 1 September, everything will be ready, but perhaps it will be later, around the 15th; I won't keep you waiting much longer.

Forgive this exasperating, useless, stupid letter.

I send you and Elly lots of love and kisses,

M. Blecher

ROMAN, 29 AUGUST 1935

My Dear Geo Bogza,

At last, I've finished *Exercises*. I think I'll manage to type everything up by 1 September, so basically the whole manuscript is pretty much complete. I had an idea : how about if I send it to you in Râșnov straight away so you have all the time and peace and quiet you need to read it at your leisure? You wrote to me that you were staying there till 15 September, so you would have enough time to read it in those tranquil surroundings, unless you're too busy writing about the Quadrilateral.[30] And after you've read it, perhaps you could pop over to Roman so that we can discuss the details of its publication.

In any case, I don't risk anything when posting the manuscript because I have another copy. So please let me know if you approve of my idea.

Sending you and Elly all my love,

M. Blecher

[30] South Dobruja in Bulgaria; Geo Bogza had a series of reportages titled "Cadrilater" that ran in *Vremea* in 1935.

ROMAN, 7 SEPTEMBER 1935

Dear Geo Bogza,

Finally, after waiting impatiently for a week, I have received a few lines from you today. At your request I'm enclosing the manuscript. Please be as critical as you like, don't hold back to spare my feelings; I'm sure I can handle it.

The text has ended up being shorter than I thought it would, about one hundred typed pages. But when printed in a larger font I imagine it will be closer to two hundred. Here is my answer to your question as to whether I fully believe in it. In principle, of course not, but in reality, I've pored over it for so many days and edited it so many times that I'm loath to make any further changes. But I know everything can be improved and even transformed, so if you come across anything that doesn't seem to work I will certainly change it, either by sticking a note on the original manuscript or even rewriting the whole page. If you notice any malapropisms, obscure phrasings, or lack of coherence (for example, if I mention at the beginning of a chapter that it's spring and then suddenly it's autumn), you must let me know. In fact, please pay close attention to this as it is entirely likely that I would not have noticed such things when I was in the middle of writing.

In short : I'm more than willing to make changes to the manuscript, but I would like it to remain more or less as it is and would like to see it published this autumn. This is my overwhelming wish, my burning desire.[31]

I greatly look forward to your response and I send loving hugs to you and Elly.

M. Blecher

[31] The manuscript, *Adventures [Exercises] in Immediate Irreality*, was published by *Vremea* in early 1936.

ROMAN, 16 SEPTEMBER 1935

Dear Geo Bogza,

I thank you with all my heart for the moving telegram you sent me. I confess that although I received it in the middle of the afternoon, I read it and re-read it late into the night, as it touched me deeply and made me very happy. What matters most to me is the fact that you liked it, everything else is secondary to that. Now here is what I will dare to ask of you : please come here with Elly and stay with me for a few weeks, because your presence is as necessary to me as a balm, especially now that I feel depressed due to complications in my illness. Please do everything in your power to satisfy this immense desire of mine.

There are two things I've been looking forward to, first of all that you read *Exercises* and secondly that you come to visit me; the first wish has come true, now I'm praying the second will as well.

With lots and lots of love,

M. Blecher

ROMAN, 23 SEPTEMBER 1935

Dear Geo Bogza,

I'm writing you in a rush, the masseur is here and I don't want to keep him waiting.

Thank you very much for the interest you have shown in *Adventures in Immediate Irreality* — I've definitely settled on that title.

I think the format used for Mircea Eliade's *Asian Alchemy* will be fine, just that I think I'd like to have just 28 lines per page rather than 35, or maybe a larger font, like the one for chapter headings I and II, the table of contents, have a look at the Eliade book.

That's all that I have to say on the matter. Most of all, I want it to come out this autumn. I'll explain to you when I see you why this is so important to me and I'm sure you'll understand.

Please do everything in your power to come to see me on 1 October, perhaps you can work on your article here, you'll have all the peace and quiet you need, I can guarantee it.

Sending you and Elly lots of love and kisses,

M. Blecher

ROMAN, 27 SEPTEMBER 1935

Dear Geo Bogza,

Forgive this brief letter, I am struggling to write. I am tormented by haemorrhoids caused by the fact that I'm lying down for such long periods of time. I'm now having to lie on warm damp compresses underneath my backside. The pain is so agonising, I can barely urinate. In short, misery.

Thank you for all the effort you've put into making sure *Adventures* is on schedule. I can send you the money you mentioned, please send me a telegram when you will need it. When will you come to Roman? Do you have a particular date in mind? There is something I've been meaning to mention, please do all you can — as I'm sure you will — to ensure the printing is done as professionally as possible so that it's an attractive book. When you came to see me I mentioned I could contribute some money for this, although naturally I hope it won't be too expensive. I "don't dare" ask my folks for money, although they would gladly give it. My greatest joy would be to see the book available for sale, not so much for my own satisfaction but to put to rest my reputation as "a man who has never earned a penny in his life." Such concerns seem horribly trivial and idiotically bourgeois to me, but they seem to matter to others around me. Anyway, I have complete faith in you. I'm expressing myself badly, to have faith in someone implies taking some sort of risk, but there is another kind of faith that doesn't fit this description, for example the kind of faith I have in my parents; I don't have faith in them, I "believe" in them, *same as I believe in you* — this is a nebulous kind of faith, a feeling under control, do you see? There is something more powerful than simple faith, and its fluid binds my entire being to you. For example : when vines "lean" on a wall, do they have faith in it or is it a question of something more vital, more essential? That's how I *lean* on you.

Forgive these digressions, I must be feverish.

Thank you for everything you do for me and lots of kisses to you and Elly,

M. Blecher

ROMAN, 15 OCTOBER 1935

Dear Geo Bogza,

Please keep me up to date with the progress of the book. Forgive the imposition; every day I wait impatiently for the post, but that doesn't mean I don't realise how very busy you are or don't appreciate how much of your precious time you have already spent seeing to my affairs. What you are doing for me is beyond human understanding, no-one is more devoted or well-meaning. You know this as well as I do and you also know that without your help I wouldn't have achieved anything.

I was sorry to hear you may not be able to take the trip to Bukovina, but I still hope you'll be able to manage it.

Please forgive this impatient postcard; I'm sure you, who understands everything, will understand this too.

I'm sending kisses to you and Elly and I can't wait to see you both,

M. Blecher

ROMAN, 27 JANUARY 1936

My Dear Geo Bogza,

At last, this morning the parcel arrived with the copies of *Adventures in Immediate Irreality*. I've spent all my time since looking at each one in turn, again and again; of course, the greatest surprise was the portrait, which I find remarkable. Thank you from the bottom of my heart for all you have done for me, for all the work you have put in to making sure the book's production was of such a high standard. The Holland paper is superb. What can I say? Thank you again, the book has exceeded my expectations, it is, in other words, *perfect*.

Tomorrow I will write a few lines to Mr. Donescu[32] and I've also enclosed here a note for Perahim,[33] if you could pass it on.

And now, please clarify something for me. How should I handle review copies, post them directly to magazines and newspapers? Please let me know which ones you were planning to send to from Bucharest. I believe we decided that you would send copies to periodicals and critics, and include your business card. I think this would be the best approach.

My sister was here when the books arrived and she was

[32] C.A. Donescu (1906-90), edited *Vremea* with his brother Vladimir.

[33] Jules Perahim (born Iuliș Blumenfeld, 1914-2008), a Jewish visual artist from Bucharest involved in the early Romanian Surrealist groups, creating illustrations for *Alge*. He moved to Paris in 1969.

incredibly impressed. Tomorrow I will give copies to my friends as I don't need so many, so if you like, I could send a few back to your Bucharest address so you would have more to post to magazines.

I keep thinking about everything you've done for me. If we hadn't met, I would still be languishing in the impenetrable darkness of the most odious dilettantism.

Thank you again, hugs, kisses and all my love to you and Elly,

M. Blecher

ROMAN, 7 FEBRUARY 1936

Dear Minet,

At last, my novel *Adventures in Immediate Irreality* has been published. I would like to send you a copy but am not sure about your address. Do you live on Rue Théophraste Renaudot?

I'm happy to inform you that my book has been very well received (although, at the end of the day, why does this even matter?). It is very different from anything I've ever sent you to read. I'm currently working on a translation into French and will send some pages to Mr. Quint. Perhaps once you see them, you could let me know what you think.

One of these days I will write to Ch. A. Cingria,[34] whom I heard is a good friend of yours. I want to write an article about him for a prominent Romanian magazine. He might ask you some questions about me. Who knows what . . . maybe if I can be taken seriously.

How are you? How is your leg? Have you finished your book?

---

[34] Charles-Albert Cingria (1883-1954), Swiss writer, poet, musician, friend of Blaise Cendrars, Max Jacob, Jean Cocteau, frequent contributor to *La Nouvelle Revue Française* [*NRF*].

Write to me when you have a spare moment.

I remain forever yours,

M. Blecher

ROMAN, 11 FEBRUARY 1936

Dear Geo Bogza,

As you can see, I've only just received the postcard you sent on February 6th, in which you inform me it's your 28th birthday. I was greatly touched by this news. As well as all the abstract, metaphysical considerations, the fact is that *we're alive*, we're human beings, and we count our lives in years, in the years we have stored all our good, extraordinary, unremarkable or sad deeds. I embrace you and kiss you on both cheeks, and I hope as the year goes on you will become even more loved and needed by others. I hope your name shines *brightly*, that the world long admire you with the spontaneous sincerity of a multitude that sees its secret, ineffable desires embodied in one particular man. I've mentioned *Tempo* and your articles to the ordinary folk I've encountered in my daily life (the man who brings me fresh bread, the electrician who came to read the meter, my uncle) and — would you believe it? — they have all read them. Just the other day I said to someone : "Have you read the article 'Here Is Popa, Where Is Popa?'[35] It's very good." And the man replied : "They're all very good." Once again, I send you my warmest, most sincere greetings and please pass them on to Elly too, as she stands loyally by your side; she is the vital elixir of the most sublime morality.

Today I've also written a letter to C.A. Donescu and yesterday

[35] Bogza's article appeared in *Tempo* on 30 January 1936.

I replied to one I received from Ieronim Șerbu.[36] I think I will submit something to *Vremea*, you can decide whether it's any good. Please send me Ilarie Voronca's address in Paris. I will send him some French translations of Bacovia that I've been working on in my spare time. I'm thinking of writing a story entitled "The Tale of the Bread Oven," a fetching enough title for a story that's fairly macabre.

I also wanted to let you know that I've finished a novella I'm calling *The Crypt*, but am not very happy with its present form. I will keep rewriting it until I achieve something readable.

Aside from literary matters, last week I was very sad to see my sister ill, it was rather serious and now she is on a special diet. You know what these diets are like, you're not allowed to eat anything tasty, only crap like unsalted vegetables, so naturally you become horribly skinny and weak.

Apart from that, everything is the same. It's winter, it's cold, but my stove heats up the room nicely. I am warm and cosy, I look after my health, my treatment continues daily, and that's about it.

Lots of kisses to you and Elly.

M. Blecher

P.S. You can write your postcards in pencil, I can read it perfectly well. Thank you with all my heart, again, for the wonderful article in *Vremea*.

Here's a little anecdote about my book. Apparently two officers were overheard talking about it in front of a shop window where it was on display : "What's up with these philosophers! Why on earth would he write 'immediate irreality' rather than 'immediate reality,' plain and simple?"

---

[36] Pen name of Aron Hers Erick (1911-72), short-story writer, publicist, and cofounder of the magazine *Discobolul*.

ROMAN, 18 FEBRUARY 1936

Dear Geo Bogza,

I have an important announcement for you : in a few days I hope to start writing my new book, but it won't be a novel, rather a continuation of *Adventures*. Don't worry, I'm aware of the difficulties associated with this, but I had the idea of a sequel structured in three books (three distinct "themes" — Berck, Leysin, Techirghiol — but in essence a continuation[37]) and if I manage to complete them, all four volumes, including the one already published, will form "my life's opus." In this new book, the "adventures" will be just as dramatic, just as shocking as in the first one, whose simple tone I will try to sustain for all my work. I would appreciate hearing what you think.

Regarding *Adventures*, please give a copy to Mr. Silviu Cernea[33] from the *Naționalul nou* newspaper, which has run announcements of its release on numerous occasions.

Sending you and Elly my affectionate kisses,

M. Blecher

ROMAN, 10 MARCH 1936

Dear Geo Bogza,

It is Tuesday today and I still haven't heard a word from you. It's been more than a week since I received your last postcard. I imagine you're very busy, I read your report on the slums in last Sunday's *Tempo*. Since the recent developments, everyone here is terribly agitated by the news about war. I'm sending you a

[37] Cf. *Scarred Hearts* and *The Illuminated Burrow*.

[38] Pseudonym of Vasile Boldeanu, also editor of *Raboj* magazine (1933-35).

"sketch" I wrote a few days ago.[39] It's really only a short piece, as concise as possible. Perhaps you'll consider it worthy of publication, I don't know. If you think it is, I would like to submit it to *Azi* [Today], if they're interested. You can mention it to Petru Manoliu, but only if you like the writing, of course, otherwise just forget about it, we don't need to discuss it ever again. I think I've mentioned to you before that I would like to publish a sketch or an essay in a substantial magazine like *Azi* because I would want to send a copy to someone abroad.[40]

Anyway, this is neither urgent nor important. I wanted to tell you that I've rented the vacant space behind the house, you know the one I mean, not on the right or left, but directly at the back of the house. At the moment it is covered with alfalfa, but I'll put in some flower beds and open a door from the hallway and create a shady terrace where I can sit during the summer (there is shade all day) protected from flies. I think it's a good idea. When you come to visit me — when? — you'll find everything ready.

In case you're interested in news from town, I can tell you that there are all sorts of scandals involving Mrs. Haymovici. The "Zionists" and Jabotinsky's followers are at loggerheads, a storm in a teacup really, and various articles and pamphlets have appeared attacking Mrs. Haymovici, but it's impossible for me to get my hands on any of them.[41]

---

[39] "Ioniță Cubiță," which remained with Bogza and was published posthumously.

[40] *Azi* was a monthly literary magazine with a socialist, anti-fascist orientation appearing from 1932 to 1938. Petru Manoliu (1903-76), a novelist, essayist, and translator, served as its editor during 1935-37.

[41] Blecher is referring to a conflict within Roman's Jewish community between mainstream Zionists and radical supporters of Ze'ev Jabotinsky's "evacuation plan" for Jews to Palestine, a plan not officially supported by the Zionist Organization under Chaim Weizmann and many Jewish communities in the region. S. Haymovici, the father of Blecher's friend Sandu, became president of the Jewish Community of Roman in 1930, thus his wife was targeted by a smear campaign.

As for my health, I'm doing well now; this sunshine has lifted my spirits a little. I'm terribly afraid of the heat and flies in the summer.

Thank you for *Rampa*; I wanted to write a few lines of gratitude to Mihail Sebastian, but I could only find the address of the printers listed.[42]

Regarding the literary projects I mentioned to you, I haven't finalized anything yet. I will write more about them later.

That's all for today.

Sending you my love and kisses, to you and Elly, yours,

M. Blecher

P.S. Please let me know if you gave a book to Silviu Cernea.

ROMAN, 11 JUNE 1936

My dear Geo Bogza,

Everything is good as long as our friendship remains unchanged. This is something that has been troubling me over the past few days, partly because of the things I mentioned in my previous letter, partly because of your recent silence. But when I received your letter today, all my misery dissipated (until now it had formed the background of my daily existence, casting a melancholy light over everything I did).

Now I can write to you in more detail about the new book.

I've written about 450 pages in notebooks and I think that I've got about 50-60 pages to go, so I'm likely to finish the first draft by next week.

It is written in the third person, so all of the characters, events

[42] *Rampa* was a Bucharest-based arts broadsheet in existence from 1911 to 1948, publishing six days a week until the final two years. Mihail Sebastian's review of *Adventures in Immediate Irreality* appeared on 22 February 1936.

and settings will be described from an objective point of view. What I am most after is to create a good, readable book, but I assume this sounds too vague to you, so I will explain what I mean.

I'm very sorry you can't come to Roman to read some of it. You already know it's set in Berck, in the world of the sick. You might remember my reasoning as to why I didn't want to shift the setting to Romania.

Well, I think you'll be pleased, I've written it in such a way that the atmosphere is not specifically French. It documents the human condition, relevant to anyone, anywhere. Even when choosing the characters' names I made sure they are universal. I'm certain you understand what I mean. I don't want the reader to think about where these events are taking place, I want them to focus only on the incidents and cases described. The story is so crammed with cruel, devastating, real life details that I think I will have to cut some of them. In *Adventures*, I wrote about the panopticon, the cinema and autumn, whereas here I'm dealing with much more serious, overwhelming aspects of life such as operating theatres, white rooms where patients wait to have their dressing changed, cold, terrifying clinics and romances between lovers encased in plaster casts. There is a hallucinatory passage where a beautiful young woman has her leg amputated, which is then taken to the basement to be incinerated. Anyway, you'll see for yourself. I want to be worthy of your friendship and your faith in me. I want to write a good book — that's all I can think about, obsessively.

On another topic, when you pass by the *Vremea* offices, I'd be truly grateful if you could pop in to ask how my book's doing, how many copies have sold, sales revenue, just so that I can get a clear idea. Also, if you bump into Mihail Sebastian, ask when he's planning to visit me in Roman and insist that he do so.

As for you, you know full well how impatiently I wait for you and Elly to come to see me. Until then, I'm sending you kisses and all my love,

M. Blecher

ROMAN, 16 JUNE 1936

Dear Mr. Ieronim Șerbu,

I wanted to thank you for the beautiful article you wrote about my book in the Easter edition of *Vremea*. I'm sorry it took me so long to write you; lately I've been preoccupied with other matters and have had little time for literature.

I've followed with great interest the instalments of your story in the most recent editions of *Vremea*.[43] It is very deep, very sad. As a veteran patient, I recognised some of the aspects of the experience that you so admirably describe and am impressed by your intuition. I think at the heart of your story is a perfect understanding of sanatorium life and your central character's inner world is vividly drawn.

There is something else I wanted to ask you about.

I wondered if you could do me a *big*, a massive favour. In our town there is a cabman, a simple man, but very honest and kind, who contracted tuberculosis a few months ago and now needs to go to the sanatorium in Bisericani.

I believe you know the sanatorium's doctor, perhaps you are even friends. I was wondering if you could write a letter of

[43] Şerbu's narrative "Flux şi reflux" [Flux and Reflux] was about the world of sanatoria (his father had contracted tuberculosis) and was serialized in *Vremea* over May and June 1936.

recommendation for this poor sick man. He has a wife and four children, an expensive domestic situation for a man who earns so little, and he deserves all the help we can give him. I think having such a letter in hand when he arrives at the sanatorium would give the man some confidence. You might not believe in the power of these "letters," but having lived in various sanatoria for many years, I can assure you they have an enormous effect on a patient's state of mind, giving them a sense of "protection" and that they will be in good hands. I really hope you do not feel offended by my request, but if so, forget I even mentioned it. The man's name is Avram Valdman [sic].

I look forward to your answer and thank you in advance.

Kind regards,

M. Blecher

ROMAN, 16 JUNE 1936

Dear Mr. Sașa Pană,

I want to ask you to do me a great favour, if you can. There is a cabman here in town, a very honest and kind man, a father to four children, who has fallen ill with T.B. and he needs to go to Bisericani. I know that you spend your summers in Piatra and was wondering if you knew the sanatorium's physician. If you do, would you please write a brief letter of recommendation for this patient. His name is Avram Waldmann. You would do me a great service and having such a "note" in hand will improve the man's morale.

I am still under the spell of those splendid drawings you showed me and hope to see you again soon.

Your friend,

M. Blecher

ROMAN, 22 JUNE 1936

Dear Mr. Ieronim Șerbu,

I wanted to let you know what an incredible impact your letter to the director of the sanatorium has had. You have made a real difference to the life of a miserable man.

Thank you with all my heart,

M. Blecher

[ROMAN], 26 JUNE 1936

Dear Geo Bogza,

Finally, I feel able to write this very long letter that I've held inside for some time, a letter that has rewritten itself so many times (in my mind) that I can't tell whether it will be able to render precisely the tone of the despair and misery I've felt on certain days. Everything feels a bit less intense at the moment, perhaps due to my lethargy or maybe because I've been absorbed in the book I've been writing, which I will tell you more about below. Either way, although I've managed to regain some relative tranquillity, I still depend on you to solve certain problems for me and give me your seal of approval.

I will write to you about anodyne and important things, jumbled together in the order I have jotted them down, as they happened

First of all, I need to tell you about an article I sent to *Vremea* straight after you left and which still hasn't been published, nor do I think it ever will be. It was about Russian philosopher Nikolai Berdyaev's ideas on *communion and collective existence* discussed in his book *Solitude and Society* [1934], in which he argues that social understanding can be achieved through spiritual and divine communion. The conclusion of my article was that such communion was only possible in material terms, I mean through work, humanity, justice, *concrete* forms of spirituality, or something like that.

Here is why I think my essay was declined for publication : firstly, because my introduction was rather obscure and unclear. I began by drawing comparisons between postwar philosophy and literary avant-garde movements, including Dadaism, pointing out the similarities between them. But perhaps I failed to put enough emphasise on the fact that their main commonality was their irrationalism, so I imagine my comparison must have seemed odd.

Secondly, I believe the timing of the article was wrong "ideologically"; *Vremea* has lately been publishing essays like "Why I Am a Patriot" and others in that vein that are profoundly antithetical to my concept of communion in materiality. (Please excuse all the deletions, the radio is broadcasting a school celebration and the awful blare has invaded my brain.)

The other thing about my article is that in the last or second-to-last issue of *Vremea* there was an article by Şuluţiu[44] about a book by Berdyaev (a different one), where Berdyaev was given favourable treatment. Might the non-publication of my article be connected to the publication of this one? I don't think so, but I would like to know why mine was rejected.

But I beg you, don't mention any of this to *Vremea*, I'm pretty much over it now, even though I was fairly upset and deflated at first. But perhaps you won't write to *Vremea* at all, especially when you see their issues praising Italy's military campaign in Abyssinia and suchlike.

---

[44] Octav Şuluţiu (1909-49), novelist, literary critic, translator.

In any case, other more important events have since occurred, so this is not worth dwelling on. And maybe the article is just bad and I didn't realise it, but I would still like you to read it.

On a similar note, *Azi* came out last month, and still without the essay I sent to Zaharia Stancu.[45] Rereading it, though, it didn't seem very "publishable" to me, so the blow wasn't quite as bitter.

And now, for more serious matters.

I wanted to tell you that Sașa Pană has visited me a few times; he's currently posted as a medic on the Buhăiești-Roman railway line and often comes this way for inspection.[46] But I better write down the details of all these visits before I give you my commentary.

One Friday afternoon a few weeks ago, my father came at 3:30, accompanied by a gentleman with glasses who introduced himself as Sașa Pană. He had my old address, so he first went to the store on the street and came back with my father.

As he was already running late after searching for me in town, he said he couldn't stay more than half an hour, until 4 o'clock, but since he now knew my address and had business around here most Fridays, he would come again next week. What was I to say? I was very embarrassed, as I will explain in more detail, but I told him I would be expecting him.

During our short time together, we talked about entirely insignificant matters, about the books I've been reading and the

[45] (1902-74), novelist, poet, philosopher and managing director of *Azi* who served as the postwar director of the National Theatre in Bucharest and president of the Writers' Union of Romania.

[46] In his commentary to their correspondence, Pană describes his visits to Blecher : "I would take the train to Roman on a Friday or Saturday morning and spend around twelve hours with him. We talked about literature and lunched together. By the bed where he lay suffering. One time, in response to my well wishes, he answered : 'Welcome to my death bed.' "

book I'm writing (which we discussed and I read him a few pages . . . but wait, you'll see . . . you'll see . . .).

I'm continuing this letter today, Friday. Yesterday, while I was writing it, Mr. Popovici stopped by and interrupted me.

After Pană had left, I deeply regretted reading him the excerpt, but that was nothing compared to the emotional turmoil I was in, aware that I'm your friend and convinced that I can't be his friend at the same time due to the falling out between you and him. It's true I did absolutely nothing to encourage his visit, and last year when he wanted to see me, I wrote him that I was too ill. Do you remember? I like straightforward situations, devoid of ambiguities, and since you're my whole meaning and joy in life, I only want to be friends with the people you befriend, to share your feelings and preferences.

But what was I to do? I confess that it's impossible for me to be unkind to someone who comes to see me. I'm just too weak, a great coward. I know it, and it torments me. I'm waiting for you to upbraid me, as I deserve.

Now to return to Sașa Pană and his visits.

In preparation for the following Friday, I pondered how to be as impersonal as possible while remaining polite. Eventually I found a solution : I invited both him and the poet Manolescu over,[47] so they spent the entire time talking while I merely listened or occasionally interjected a word. In any case, I was fiercely determined not to read anything anymore nor even mention my book, and I held to it.

---

[47] Ion Sofia Manolescu (1909-93), noted poet in Roman and close friend of Blecher. Pană agreed to publish his poetry collection *Odihna neagră* (Bucharest : Editura Unu, 1936), commenting : "publishing expenses were shared by the author and the publisher."

But then another thing happened : Manolescu brought along his poems, read them aloud, Pană liked them, and so we all agreed they should be published by Unu.

And now I must pause again as I anticipate your reproaches and disdain for what I've done. I'm writing this with immense bitterness; every time I think of your reading these lines it feels like burning coals in my heart. But I've decided to tell you everything, to confess everything, I don't want to hide anything from you, and even if I have to face your disdain (which would be terrible, the most terrible thing in my life), I had to come clean so that I can carry on being honest with you.

I feel a deep sense of indifference towards everyone else in the world, an indifference I hide as I speak, write, or act in their company. But when it comes to you, I lose all clarity, and I feel everything related to you is melted into my blood, roaring within me, vibrating within me, indiscernibly mixed with my own being.

The truth is that my life is what it was before I met you *plus* what you have made of it.

Returning to the aforementioned visits, it was decided that Pană would come again the following Friday and finalise everything for the publication of the poetry collection, which would be in autumn, but printed in summer. So Pană will bring samples when he returns on Friday, 3 July, and Manolescu will contribute 1000 lei for paper and printing. The book will cost 4000 lei in total and should be beautifully printed on high-quality paper.

Please consider for a moment that for Manolescu it is an extraordinary opportunity to have the printing, layout, and publicizing in the magazine of his book handled by Sașa Pană, and he is overjoyed, floating in a state of utter bliss, that it will be published by Editura Unu. It will even have an illustration by H. Maxy,[48] so he's simply beside himself with delight.

So that's the Sașa Pană situation. Everything I've written you only conveys a faint echo of all my internal torments (yes, torments) regarding this terrible, dreadful emotional dilemma that has caught me between my friendship for you and my natural tendency to behave kindly and amiably towards everyone. Feel free to condemn my cowardice.

When I left Techirghiol and came to Brașov, where we discussed all the tribulations I went through in the sanatoria and I was calmed by your empathetic responses, I believed I had now left my unrest behind, or "stuff" as you put it, and that in a calm, composed manner I could focus solely on my health and the books I wanted to write. But now there are other anxieties and other sorrows. My life has not been characterised by inner solace, and now I receive everything like someone who has suffered so many blows he has grown accustomed to them and is waiting for new ones to strike somehow and somewhere. I've achieved a technical proficiency in these matters, becoming a professional in them, and now the impatience with which I await your response throws a veil of despair over everything.

But maybe, *maybe* you will forgive me, absolve me, I think (and maybe this is right) that you see all this from above, as if from an airplane, a 1000 meters high, and none of it is important to you. In other words, you won't mind that I was friendly to Sașa Pană and that Manolescu is being published by Unu. Still, I believe that things are too serious . . . too tangled . . . I await your response.

I have a little space left to write to you about the book I'm writing, a novel called *Scar Tissue*,[49] where I talk about the

[48] Max Hermann Maxy (1895-1971), Romanian modernist visual artist.

[49] The first version of *Scarred Hearts*, extant in Blecher's notebooks.

gloomy life of patients in Berck. Perhaps you won't like the title at first, but once you've read the book, you'll see that it really suits the content and will then make sense to you. So far I've written four thick notebooks filled with pure happenings, closely interconnected, unsweetened by superfluous sentimentality, peppered with some virulent, bitter things. I want the book to be devastating.

But the notebooks (and I want to tell you this specifically, in case something happens and I might not be able to transcribe them) contain only the first version, written hastily, and I still need to correct many passages. I'm writing to you in such haste about the book because I want to read you a few pages first. I believe and hope it will be worthy of the trust you have placed in me. Some passages are infinitely more poignant and startling than in *Adventures*. Anyway, you will see.

Two more bits of news : my health is good and I've been learning to play the accordion, that's all.

I conclude with immense restlessness and impatience, awaiting your reply. I'm not asking for a long letter, a few words on a postcard will do, and I will understand if everything is good between us or if I should continue to wallow in the same bitterness and despair.

Sending you and Elly many kisses,

M. Blecher

ROMAN, 12 [JULY] 1936

Dear Minet,

I know you can't be bothered to write to me, but yesterday morning I found in the July edition of the *NRF* a few lines from Ch. A. Cingria, which reminded me that you are friends, and I was wondering if you would do me a favour, when you have the time, and ask him if he has received my letter.

Please understand, I have no interest in pressuring him to reply, I would only like some reassurance because my letters have been strangely getting lost of late.

That's all for this morning, I am writing a new book, but please believe me that in no way am I a "man of letters."

This was the most pressing thing I wanted to tell you.

Yours,

M. Blecher

ROMAN, 3 AUGUST 1936

Dear Mr. Sașa Pană,

Thank you very much for the bottle you sent, which was delivered to me yesterday. It is exactly what I wanted.

I am sending you a money order for the 500 lei I received from Ion Manolescu (he has given me money for safekeeping because there is a fair in Roman and he can't resist all the temptations . . . he dropped several hundred lei on some trick the other night . . . that's what it means to have poetry in your blood).

Please let me know when you're leaving for Piatra and the address where you'll be staying because I have a small parcel for your son, Vladimir, and since it contains some ceramics objects I made, I don't want to risk posting it.

If you'll allow it, I would be delighted to befriend your son.

My warmest regards,

M. Blecher

ROMAN, 21 AUGUST 1936

Dear Geo Bogza,

Please let me know the exact date of your departure as I would like to send a few pages of my manuscript to Mihail Sebastian so that he can show them to his editor, and I would very much like you to have a look at them first. If you're too busy to reply to me right away, I will ask Mihail to let you know when he receives the manuscript and pass it on to you.

I have to confess that I'm in a dark mood at the moment, bored of everything and only persevering with the book because I need to finish what I've started as well as for . . . the usual reasons, which I can better explain to you when I see you.

Please let me know if the fire has caused much destruction and if you've suffered significant losses.

Lots of kisses and much love to you and Elly,

M. Blecher

[ROMAN], 20 SEPTEMBER 1936

Dear Mr. Sașa Pană,

I deeply regret to inform you that I won't be able to do the translations I have promised you.

All week long I have been tormented by various aches that are still bothering me and I haven't been able to write a single sentence.[50] You will see the state I'm in when you come to visit me on Friday and I'm sure you'll understand.

With warm regards,

M. Blecher

---

[50] A couple of weeks earlier Blecher fell out of his cart and broke several bones.

ROMAN, 29 SEPTEMBER 1936

Dear Geo Bogza,

At last, I'm in a position to send you some news about myself and the book. Yesterday Mihail Sebastian came to see me and took my manuscript back to Bucharest. He read some of it while he was with me and said he liked it very much. I'm sure you'll ask him about it. This is his address : 19 Radu Vodă Street, phone number 46846, although I expect he will phone you first.

Now please be patient as you read the following lines. So, when Mihail said he was coming to see me, I really wanted to finish the manuscript before he arrived, and for the last six days I edited it every morning, afternoon and night until 3-4 a.m. By the time I finished, I was absolutely exhausted, broken, drained of all energy; it took an enormous amount of physical effort to complete this manuscript, I really overstretched myself.

I expect Mihail will tell you how haggard I looked after all this work as it really took its toll on my body, especially my aching hips.

Anyway, at least I've finished it, but I wanted to make sure you don't mind that I've sent it straight to the editor. I have to confess, it would drive me crazy with worry to think these pages I've slaved over were being circulated around Bucharest and could possibly get lost. Forgive me, condemn me, but understand me.

I know how impatient and curious you have been to see the manuscript — talk to Mihail and he'll let you take a quick look at it, and give you an overview of the whole thing as well. Please ask him if there are any saccharine moments or pointless episodes . . . He'll tell you everything.

This is as much as I can write to you today. I'm very tired and can't continue, but please, I ask you again, forgive me.

Love and kisses to you and Elly,

M. Blecher

P.S. I'll write you a longer letter soon about some important issues.

ROMAN, 23 NOVEMBER 1936

Dear and great Geo Bogza,

Today, at last, I've received from you the lines I've been waiting to read. Admittedly, I've been impatient.

Something has come between us recently, something I can't easily define, perhaps related to your disappointment or my indolence. When something so absolutely preoccupies me, when I feel unsettled, I can't put my mind to anything else, no matter how essential or urgent : I was completely annihilated, vanquished by stupid anticipation. The last few days have been spent waiting for *Scarred Hearts,* as per agreement with the publisher.

Mihail Sebastian will explain to you the details of the book's publication. I think you can probably guess that it wasn't a smooth process, and now that it will finally arrive in bookshops the smile on my face will not be of satisfaction, but the weary smile of having just endured a difficult labour.

These are the reasons why I haven't managed to write to you. But taking stock of them now, I confess to being humbled at how petty they are compared to your own much more serious and very real troubles "from life, not from books" at this time, such that I want to hide in shame.[51]

Granted, I haven't had it easy myself, for reasons that have

[51] See earlier mention of Bogza's continuing legal troubles from his work being labeled pornographic.

nothing to do with literature. I've had a few complications relating to my illness which have caused me a lot of hardship and pain, but I feel that nothing compares to the demoralising despair that gnaws at your heart like a nest of mice.

You know I don't believe in supernatural forces, but if such forces were to exist, I would like them to transfer all your misery and sadness to me, so that I could gladly suffer in your place, feeling your pain piercing my flesh rather than imagining you in torment. Perhaps you'll dismiss this wish as naive, this is always the way with anything deeply felt, any thought capable of consuming your days and nights : as soon as you write about such feelings, they appear naive . . .

And yet this is the last thought in my mind as I go to sleep and which I harbour not only in my heart, but in my entire being.

Look : if this piece of paper and this promise have any meaning, much of which is in realms we cannot fathom, starting from today I want to take upon myself all your despair, disquiet and suffering.

Please, dear Bogza, give careful consideration to everything I write to you and don't make fun of it. (In fact, nothing in the world is ridiculous, apart from a few bourgeois things that deserve only a hoot of laughter.)

And now, let's move on to happier topics.

When are you and Elly coming to visit me? I think I've already mentioned that I have an accordion and I play it almost every day. It's a splendid musical instrument — I'm referring here to my accordion, not to the instrument in general — decorated with celluloid and nickel, with keys like on a piano, capable of producing the most astonishing notes. I'm always practising, hoping that I can improve; at the moment, I think my playing is passable.

Everything else here is still painted in the same dull, grey tones of a monotonous, solitary life. Today it snowed and there was a white, unusual light in the room. I've moved to the room in the centre of the house for the winter months, just like last year. Everything around me has been arranged just as before.

It would be wonderful if you could come over for an extended stay. We would be as tight as we were in Brașov — let's allow ourselves to be utterly selfish and absorbed in our friendship, to live a few "pure" days.

But I know this is just my daydream, that it cannot happen in reality . . .

I'm sending you my love, warmer and more vital than ever before, like a wine improved with age,

M. Blecher

[ROMAN], 9 DECEMBER 1936

Dear Mr. Sașa Pană,

Manolescu has just been to see me, I understand the lads have been looking for him at work and at home but didn't manage to catch him. He tells me he sent you 700 lei — he still owes you another 700 and will send it to you at the beginning of next month.

I'm sure this delay is an inconvenience, but please give Manolescu some leeway. I will see to it that he sends you the money as promised.

With warm regards,

M. Blecher

ROMAN, 18 DECEMBER 1936

Dear Mr. Ocneanu,

I've just received the first copy of *Scarred Hearts*[52] and I'm very satisfied with the typography as well as the cover. Many thanks for the attention and care you have given it to ensure such high quality production. In addition to the journals you have mentioned to me, please also send review copies to the following :

Mr. Octav Șuluțiu, 6 Lunca Plăeșului, Brașov (for *Familia* magazine);

Mr. Mihail Chirnoagă, 3 Ianov Street, Iași (he writes a column for *Pamantul*);

Mr. Ion Biberi, (from the newspaper *Le Moment*);[53]

Mr. Geo Bogza, (for *Tempo*).

I will write Mr. Bogza to pick up his copy himself so that it doesn't get mislaid in the editorial office. Please also send me my author's copies.

Many thanks for everything and kind regards,

M. Blecher

ROMAN, 18 DECEMBER 1936

Dearest Geo Bogza,

I wanted to let you know that my book has finally come out and please forgive that I haven't written to you until now — I was so paralysed by the anticipation of its publication I couldn't do

[52] Published on Mihail Sebastian's suggestion by Alcalay in Bucharest in early 1937, but printed in late 1936; Emil Ocneanu was the director of the publishing house.

[53] Mihail Chirnoagă (1913-48), literary critic and author of short prose; Ion Biberi (1904-90), prose writer, essayist, and literary critic.

anything, and it also made me realise that I can't control my nerves.

Anyway, the book is now lying on the table. It's reminded me once again how much you have done for me and all I owe you. You were the one who raised me up from my state of decay and set me on the right path. Thank you so much, my dear Geo Bogza, and also thank you dear Elly, your admirable presence has always sustained the atmosphere of friendship between me and Geo. Your presence has been a perfect complement to our friendship, purely, you are as necessary to it as air is to life. I love you both and can't wait to see you. This is what I wanted to write to you : I would like you to come and stay with me for a month, you will live here worry-free and Geo can regain his zest for life, which I feel has been sadly depleted of late. Please, do come. I think it will be the best thing for you both, as well as for me, I urgently need you close to me, I crave your love and your clarity of thought. Please come. I think Geo could arrange a leave of absence from *Tempo* for a month; he could file articles from here. Anyway, give it some serious thought and think especially about the joy it would give me.

My dears, I have set aside a copy of the book for you; it's printed on Japan paper and I will give it to you when you come. Until then, if you want to read it, I'd be grateful if Geo could pick up a copy from Alcalay, I've already let them know.

I look forward to seeing you, with love, with ardent love.

Yours,

M. Blecher

P.S. Sorry for the sign-off.

ROMAN, 1 JANUARY 1937

Dear Geo Bogza,

It's midnight, they have just fired the gun in town and woke me up in the process; so this is the start of a new year, and my first thoughts are of you and Elly. I send hugs and warmest, loving regards to you both.

I've received everything you sent me, but please forgive me because recently I've been very busy.

Mihail Sebastian stayed with me for two days [last week] and I've had a few other visits recently — seeing him has brought me a great deal of joy, he calms me and I feel he understands me to the very depths of my soul.

When will you and Elly come to Roman? I wanted to send you something, but didn't manage it because Fridy, who takes care of these things for me, is now quite ill. Mihail will tell you what's wrong with her, if you ask him.

Hugs and kisses to you and Elly. Thank you for all your letters. As I read them I experienced the deepest emotions I have ever felt in my life,

M. Blecher

ROMAN, 12 JANUARY 1937

Dear Geo Bogza,

I'm sending you this letter by registered mail because I suspect a number of my postcards have got lost in the post.

Are you sure you're receiving all your mail at your new address? Investigate and let me know.

Please don't worry, everything here is fine, I'm fine and nothing has prevented me from writing to you.

A few days ago I received a postcard from you in which you expressed your surprise at my "silence" — but I've been writing to you all this time, especially in reply to your extraordinary letters, which have shaken me to the core.

I hope you don't mind, but I read some lines from them to my father, and he was moved to tears.

It is superfluous to remind you that I live for these lines from you, that they are my lifeblood. These heartfelt testaments of friendship are the only things that make my life bearable.

Meeting you and Elly has been the most extraordinary experience of my life, as you certainly know — but perhaps you don't understand this completely, because you cannot hear the murmur of love for you that resonates in every cell of my body, the murmur of blood that creates the very melody of love.

Sorry for these lines, I only write what passes through my mind, I mean I only write what emerges from my very depths.

With frenetic love and many kisses,

M. Blecher

[ROMAN], 3 FEBRUARY 1937

Dear Mr. Sașa Pană,

Thank you for your kind thoughts. I have received a letter from Tiberiu Iliescu[54] and Al. Assan asking for a submission to *Meridian* but I have nothing suitable to send them. I agree with you that *Meridian* is a good magazine, it's just a shame about the typos. In the review of Manolescu's book they wrote "ballag" instead of "ballad." Why not "baligă" (excrement)? These flaws mar the prestige of the magazine. Encourage them to avoid such

[54] (1906-78), author of short prose and publicist, but primarily the editor in chief of the Craiova-based modernist magazine *Meridian* (1934-46). Apparently Blecher's concern about the plethora of typos dissuaded him from submitting to it.

mistakes and then *Meridian* would be not merely a good magazine, but an excellent one.

Fondly,

M. Blecher

P.S. Please keep me up to date with everything you receive from André Breton; I'm very interested.

BUCHAREST, 10 MAY 1937

[To Pierre Minet,]

. . . . you must be in touch with . . . . Ilarie Voronca. I am . . . . in Bucharest,[55] where I had to travel urgently on account of an enormous abscess on my thigh that has been tormenting me for over a month.[56] Anyway, everything has been more or less sorted out, the abscess has been lanced and I feel a little better.

I don't have your letter here with me, but I wanted to tell you how much your words touched me — I'll come back to this later.

I am writing you these lines only to convey my eternal friendship.

M. Blecher

P.S. Send your letters to Roman, they will be brought to me by courier.

P.P.S. Please give my best wishes to Mr. Voronca.

ROMAN, 23 JUNE 1937

Dear Minet,

I've just received your letter. I don't intend to write much, but

---

[55] Lacunae in the original.

[56] In early May 1937, Blecher began treatment at the Saint Vincent de Paul Sanatorium in Bucharest.

I just wanted to tell you that it's one of the most rare and exquisite things in the world to have a friend like you. Thank you for taking an interest in my translations. This is what I intend to do — I will take it upon myself to translate my first book[57] (I've already started) because it is the most difficult to translate and it features particular nuances and expressions that I want to convey in French in "my own style."

I will send it to you and you can do with it whatever you like.

Wauquier will go through it first, editing the grammar and syntax. He will also type it up.

I think it will take me two months, more or less, to get it finished. I can't do it any faster than that because I want to make sure the final result is of a high quality.

I regret I can't work more intensively at the moment — I'm suffering from enteritis and feel absolutely drained — but as soon as I feel better I will be able to work harder, at least I hope so.

From now on write to me in Roman, it's the most reliable address.

I will probably go to the mountains for a few weeks.

Forever yours, sincerely,

M. Blecher

ROMAN, 15 JULY 1937

My dear Mr. Voronca,

In the latest edition of *Les Nouvelles littéraires* I read a poem of yours that brought so much light and joy into my lonely afternoon that I wanted to thank you from the bottom of my heart. It is the most serene and beautiful thing I have read in a long while.

[57] Blecher's own French translation of *Adventures in Immediate Irreality*, which he hoped Minet would help to get published.

I am sending you these lines along with all my gratitude and friendship,

M. Blecher

P.S. Please give my regards to your wife.

ROMAN, 22 JULY 1937

Dear Mr. Ieronim Șerbu,

Thank you very much for defending me in your article in *Lumea Românească* [Romanian World]. I have to confess that I'm not familiar with the article in *Facla* [The Torch][58] you mention since the publication is not available in my town. I would be grateful if you could send me a copy.

It's embarrassing to know that I've been attacked without knowing the details; they might be expecting me to defend myself and think I haven't done so out of . . . cowardice.

You would be doing me a great service if you could send me the magazine, and please don't worry that it will upset me. I think I possess enough moral fortitude to cope with an attack on my literary work, no matter how vicious.

Many thanks again, and sending you all my best,

M. Blecher

ROMAN, 19 AUGUST 1937

Dear Geo Bogza,

Please forgive my silence for so many days, but I want you to know I haven't written till now not because I didn't think of it nor because I was short on time. Please believe me that it was

[58] In an article appearing in the magazine on 7 July 1937, the author, Oscar Lemnaru, essentially calls the "author of *Scarred Hearts*" a clown.

simply because I didn't feel capable of writing a single line. The last few days in Roman have been scorching, absolutely enervating. At last, yesterday it started to rain, so I felt able to write this letter.

If you see Mihail Sebastian, please tell him I'm sorry I haven't written to him yet. I think he would have probably worked out the reason for my prolonged silence as I wrote to him from Brașov that the heat was making me miserable.

I understand better than you can imagine the sadness you've described to me. I'm only sorry we're so in tune with each other that we share this complete desolation . . .

For a long time, literature, poetry, even reality itself have irremediably lost any kind of attraction for me, and the only reason I continue to live, to occupy my mind, to write, is because I haven't got anything better to do in my current condition.

In Berck, there is a "charitable foundation" that teaches the sick to weave baskets and knit flannels, but I can't weave baskets, nor can I knit, so I write books . . . Everything I do, the life I "live," seems like a hallucination, as if I'm in a daze after smoking opium. At the end of the day, life is just the same, a kind of sleepwalking, no matter if you're smoking opium or not. Everything I'm writing to you here is tinged with an immense sadness. This "hallucination" hasn't held any appeal or fresh interest for me for a long time now, and I'm indifferent to all its various forms.

Please forgive me for replying to your despair by offering you another version of despair in return.

When are you and Elly coming to visit me?

Hugs and lots of love to you,

M. Blecher

ROMAN, 10 MAY 1938

My dear and great Geo Bogza,

I'm writing to you after a relatively good night; around two o'clock, what needed to happen happened, although it was not the same as before. I think that I'll eat the chicken today.

Pintilie is watering the garden and when he is finished he'll go for a walk with Olimpia, whose toothache seems better today.

It's very early in the morning, it's warm and sunny outside, perhaps I will go out to the terrace.

I'm truly sorry you found me in such a miserable state yesterday, forgive me for making such a spectacle of myself, you know how much I hate playing the role of "professional patient."

How is our good and pure Elly?

I will try to write a little today and force myself to finish by the end of the month. In a week's time I will write to Sașa Pană explaining that I'm ill and he should delay his visit, without indicating any particular date. I'm hoping he will get the message and refrain from visiting me altogether. I don't think I made it clear to you yesterday that it's been exactly eight months since I wrote to him.[59] I have no interest in being labeled a Surrealist poet, just as I don't want to be a provincial author. Anyway, these kinds of subtleties should be discussed on another occasion.

Lots of love to you and Elly.

Yours,

M. Blecher[60]

---

[59] Cf. final letter to Pană above. It actually dates to 3 February 1937, so fifteen months earlier.

[60] Blecher died three weeks later, on May 31.

AN INTERVIEW WITH MAX BLECHER

His literary debut. Adventures in Immediate Irreality. *The current generation. Foreign influences on* Scarred Hearts. *A Romanian prize like the Prix Goncourt. The role of the writer in today's society. Writers that should be translated into Romanian. Current projects.*

Who is M. Blecher!

This is the question the salesclerks in the Romanian literature department of one of Bucharest's most prominent bookshops are asked every day. Despite the fact that Mr. Blecher published a poetry collection titled *Transparent Body* in 1934, and has contributed perceptive essays to *Vremea*, even though he as written a novel (*Adventures in Immediate Irreality*) of such rare quality that it can be justly described as the greatest literary success of 1936, the publication of his new book, *Scarred Hearts*, still generates questions about his identity, even from those who consider themselves to be up on Romanian literature.

Adventures in Immediate Irreality — a book that was poorly printed, poorly publicised, and with an unappealing title — was nevertheless a great critical success, of a kind we have not seen for some time in the literary world.

From the notoriously harsh critic Eugen Ionescu to the honest, highly principled Pompiliu Constantinescu, with his deep understanding of literature, everyone sang the book's praises.

And, after many years, M. Blecher, this important figure of the new generation, praised for his "authenticity," "experience" and “subtle understanding of life,” sends us from Roman the most lucid account of what it means to be human — the novel *Scarred Hearts*.

It is not the purpose here to dwell on the fact that *Adventures in Immediate Irreality* did not enjoy the success it deserved. But the presentation and launch of Mr. Blecher’s most recent book does deserve to be discussed.

The manuscript was handled by the experienced editor Emil Ocneanu, who immediately understood its value and decided he would spare no effort in the book’s publication and in establishing Mr. Blecher’s reputation as a writer.

The publication of his latest novel has prompted us to contact Mr. Blecher with a few questions that would interest the readers of *Rampa*. He replied to us from Roman, a quiet, traditional town in the north of the Moldova region, with the charm that characterises the people from his part of the country. Naturally, the first question was about his debut.

What was your literary debut?
In the summer of 1929, while I was staying in Berck, I sent a few short pieces to the magazine *Bilete de papagal*. I had been abroad a long time and didn’t know that the magazine had ceased publication. And then I forgot all about my submission. But in 1930, the magazine started up again and published the pieces I had sent them. I experienced a double pleasure then : first of all, the joy of seeing my writing in print, and secondly, the knowledge that someone had liked the pieces so much that they held onto them all that time.

It seems many young writers have gotten their start in *Bilete de papagal.* I think Tudor Arghezi[61] has achieved something noble in encouraging so many young writers. It is rare to see an established author taking the trouble to nurture the talent of the younger generation. Mr. Arghezi's sympathetic approach, combined with his rigorous criticism, has guided these young writers in the right direction. Personally, I am grateful for the support he has given me and I want to take this opportunity to express my admiration for everything he has done.

How did the publication of *Adventures in Immediate Irreality* come about?
Publication of the book was the result of my meeting Geo Bogza in Brașov in 1934, which developed into a great friendship. In my life, I have had two friendships that have had an enormous impact on me : one with Pierre Minet, whom I befriended in a sanatorium in Berck, and the other with Geo Bogza and his admirable wife, whom I also met in Brașov. At that time, I had sunk into a dreadful, overwhelming depression. I had a pile of manuscripts I didn't know what to do with, having started *Adventures* a while back. I read a few pages to Geo Bogza, and he encouraged me to finish it. Without the encouragement and companionship of these two dear friends, Geo and Elisabeta Bogza, I wouldn't have been able to write the novel. In addition to encouraging my literary aspirations, they also reawakened my lust for life, arousing new and salutary inner tensions.

Later, I moved back to Roman and finished the novel there. After that, Geo Bogza came to see me and took it back to Bucharest, where he arranged its publication. So that's the story of *Adventures*.

[61] The pseudonym of Ion N. Theodorescu (1880-1967), born in Bucharest, editor of *Facla* before taking charge of *Bilete de papagal.*

(There have been some heated debates of late about the new generation, similar to the debates that raged on many years before about the previous generation, who are no longer in the bloom of youth. I asked Mr. Blecher, a man who has removed himself from the bustle of modern life, to share his opinion on the new generation.)

What do you think about the "new generation"?
I detest such vague terms and overgeneralisations. I've always considered boundaries between generations and literary groups to be a somewhat artificial construct. I do believe, however, in a zeitgeist of this particular age, as it has its own unique spiritual preoccupations and intentions. This is because the challenges facing people today are particularly tough and require more radical solutions.

If I may borrow the phrase of a French writer, I would say that the restlessness of today's youth is characterized by the disproportionate growth of "literary aggression."

(I asked Mr. Blecher about what influence foreign writers such as Kessel, Mann et al. have had on his latest novel.)

Did any of these foreign writers influence *Scarred Hearts*?
I'm not sure. We pour everything we have seen, read and lived into our writing. I would say that the events in *Scarred Hearts* are more closely related to my life experiences than to other books. I was dealing with material that was presented to me in such a compact, overwhelming form that it would have been difficult to squeeze any literary influences into the narrative.

In Romania, our only literary prizes are awarded by the Union of Romanian Writers and by the publishing house National Culture. Ideally, we would also have something akin to the Goncourt Prize, which would be awarded by the Association of Romanian Publishers. If such a prize were to exist, who do you think should win it?
You're putting me on the spot here. Please accept my apologies, but I have no answer.

What is the role of the writer in our current age?
The writer should climb down from the "ivory tower" and join the "forum." The point of view of intellectuals should be easily grasped by anyone who is interested in their work, as their purpose is to shed light on important issues and guide the masses who are interested in the opinions of *today's intellectual*.

At the moment I'm feeling rather sceptical about the "general" importance of literature. Does a writer have any real influence? I doubt it, and I can't think of many examples in history when society was changed by novels or writers' opinions. But possibly things are different now, perhaps people are reading more and making use of the knowledge they've gained. If this is the case, then of course, a writer who is aware of what is going on in the world should try to bring about social change by making an ideological contribution. However, this contribution must be in keeping with their integrity as a writer, their skills employed to promote justice and spiritual freedom. It is rather sad that these days some writers only climb down from their "ivory tower" to bring venom and blind political passions to the table, their voices only adding confusion, abstruse ideas and intolerance to the general debate — rather than taking on the conciliatory role we might expect from them. Yes, it's rather sad that these "intellectuals" fuel virulence and violence at a time when it's in such abundance already.

Our country's literature is not being translated into universal languages because some argue that it has nothing to offer to the foreign reader. Which Romanian writers ought to be translated into other languages?

First of all Rebreanu, then some novels by Sadoveanu and Mircea Eliade, as well as some interesting essays and works by Tudor Vianu and C. Noica.[62] But there are many other interesting books that ought to be translated.

Any new projects?

At the moment I'm working on a novel set partly in a small provincial town as well as in Switzerland.[63] I can't tell you much more about it because that's pretty much all I know right now.

While living in Roman, Mr. Blecher is writing a book that echoes this passage from *Scarred Hearts* :

> A book is a nothing, it's not even an object. It's something dead . . . that contains living things, like a putrefying body swarming with thousands and thousands of insects.

---

[62] Liviu Rebreanu (1885-1944), novelist, playwright, journalist, considered the founder of the modern Romanian novel post-WWI; Mihail Sadoveanu (1880-1961), journalist, novelist, politician; Tudor Vianu (1898-1964), literary and art critic, poet, philosopher, translator; Constantin Noica (1909-87), poet, essayist, philosopher exploring the crisis of modern culture.

[63] Cf. *The Illuminated Burrow*, which was published posthumously.

And in this new work — like any other of Mr. Blecher's books — the future reader will find that the following lines from *Scarred Hearts* still ring true :

> The book contained all the boredom, sadness, dreams and frenzy that could be found in the most fantastical, disturbingly beautiful poetry. In vain did he search his memory for another book that he could compare it to, this novel was unlike any verse or line of literature he had ever encountered before. It contained a venom that slowly, slowly dripped in his blood as he read it, making him feel lightheaded and feverish, as if a cunning, aggressive virus had invaded his body.

Gh. A. Harabagiu
Rampa, 1937

The selections were made from two major collections of Blecher's work : Max Blecher, *Opere,* edited by Doris Mironescu (Bucharest: Academia Română, 2017) [below as Collected Works]; Max Blecher, *Vizuina Luminată. Corp transparent, Proze, Publicistică, Arhivă . . . ,* edited and selected by Saşa Pană (Bucharest: Cartea Românescă, 1971) [below as Selected Works].

Being more comprehensive and recent, as well as including a wealth of helpful annotations and commentary, the Mironescu edition served as the primary source while the Pană edition served for cross reference, comparison, and additional information.

Original publications

"Transparent Body" appeared in Romanian as *Corp transparent* (Bucharest: Editura Bibliofila, 1934). "Your Hands," was originally titled "Cînd" [When], but was later changed by Blecher himself when republished in the magazine *Adam* in January 1937, and it appears under this title in Collected Works (yet under the original title in Selected Works).

"The Inextricable Position" in French as L'Inextricable position," in *Le Surréalisme au service de la révolution,* no. 6 (May 1933), and translated into Romanian by Saşa Pană as "Poziție de nedescâlcit" in *Antologie literaturii române de avangardă* (Bucharest: Editura Pentru Literatura, 1969), republished in the notes in Collected Works.

"Paris" in *Vremea,* vol. VII, no. 368 (1934), and appears in both Selected and Collected Works.

The prose poem "[for an instant]" as "[pentru o clipă]," first published posthumously from Saşa Pană's archives in Selected Works, republished in Collected Works.

"Diurnal Moment" and "Fugue" were given to Geo Bogza in 1934 and first published posthumously as "Moment Diurn" and "Fugă" in *Mozaicul,* vol. XVII, nos. 3-4 (1985-86), republished in Collected Works.

"Herrant" first appeared under this title in *Bilete de papagal,* no. 463 (29 June 1930), republished in both Selected and Collected Works.

"Don Jazz" first appeared under this title in *Bilete de papagal,* no. 465 (12 July 1930), republished in both Selected and Collected Works.

"Limits" : Originally appearing as "Limite," parts I, II, III were published in *Bilete de papagal,* respectively in three consecutive issues : no. 469 (10 August 1930); no. 470 (17 August 1930); no. 471 (24 August 1930) and republished in both Selected and Collected Works. Part IV does not appear in Selected Works and was originally sent to Ion Valerian (see letter from 16 June 1931) with three prose pieces below as submissions to his literary magazine *Viața literară*. It was ultimately published posthumously in *Manuscriptem,* vol. XIX, no. 1 (1988) and republished in Collected Works as a separate entry under "posthumous prose." We have combined it here with the other three parts of "Limits" published during Blecher's lifetime as keeping the series together seemed to make the most sense for a translated edition.

"Buțu" and "Jenică" first appeared under those titles in *Adevărul literar și artistic,* vol. XII, no. 661 (6 August 1933) and republished together in Selected Works under the heading "Portraits" and as separate entries in Collected Works.

"Ix – Mix – Fix" under this title in *Frize,* vol. I, nos. 6-7 (Brașov, August–September 1934), and appears in both Selected and Collected Works.

"Insinuations" as "Insinuări" in *Frize,* vol. I, no. 8 (Brașov, October 1934), and appears in both Selected and Collected Works.

"Berck, Kingdom of the Damned" as "Berck, orașul damnaților" in *Vremea,* vol. VII, no. 358 (October 1934), and appears in both Selected and Collected Works.

"Fever," "Mab", and "Love" resp. as "Febră," "Mab," and "Dragoste" were originally sent to Ion Valerian in 1931 for publication in *Viața literară,* which he never did. They were first published together posthumously in *Manuscriptem,* vol. XVIII, no. 4 (1987) and republished in Collected Works.

"Ioniță Cubiță" under this title was sent in March 1936 to Geo Bogza (see letter from 10 March) but never published. It appeared for the first time in *M. Blecher, mai puțin cunoscut* [M. Blecher, Lesser Known], edited by Mădălina Lascu (Bucharest: Hasefer, 2000) and republished in Collected Works.

"Aizic Wolf" under this title first appeared in Collected Works with the gloss that it is a fragmentary text taken from Blecher's first notebook.

"Selected Correspondence": since the Selected Works only includes the letters to Saşa Pană and Ilarie Voronca, our selection has come exclusively from the extensive correspondence published in Collected Works. In his edition, however, Pană does provide some interesting commentary and context to Blecher's letters to him, and some of these comments have been incorporated herein as footnotes.

"An Interview with Max Blecher" first appeared in *Rampa* on 17 February 1937, and is reprinted in both Selected and Collected Works.

BIO NOTES

MAX BLECHER was born in Botoşani, Romania, on September 8, 1909, into a middle-class Jewish family. His father owned a porcelain shop. He spent his childhood and adolescence in Roman, and upon graduating high school left for Paris to study medicine, but soon became ill and was diagnosed with spinal tuberculosis. After spending six years in various sanatoria, he returned to Roman where, confined to bed, he began to translate (Guillaume Apollinaire inter alios) and to write, contributing texts to magazines as well as corresponding with some of the leading artists and intellectuals of the day. His only collection of poetry, *Transparent Body*, was published in 1934, followed by the "novels" *Adventures in Immediate Irreality* (1936) and *Scarred Hearts* (1937). Although his final prose work, *The Illuminated Burrow*, was written in 1937-38, it was only published posthumously, first in an abridged edition in 1947, and then in full in 1971. Often described as "hallucinatory" and "nightmarish," Blecher's writing is a kindred spirit to Surrealism and a major contribution to the 20th-century European avant-garde. He died on May 31, 1938.

GABI REIGH was born in Romania and moved at the age of twelve to the UK, where she teaches English and translates. As part of her Interbellum Series she has translated a variety of work by Lucian Blaga, Liviu Rebreanu, Max Blecher, and Mihail Sebastian. A recipient of the Stephen Spender Prize in 2017, her anthology of women's writing from the early 20th century, *Virginia's Sisters*, was published in 2023.

JINDŘICH HEISLER (1914-53), a poet and visual artist, was a member of the Surrealist Group in Czechoslovakia who after moving to Paris with Toyen in 1947 was also active in the postwar French Surrealist Group.